THE GOOD SAMARITAN

THE GOOD SAMARITAN

A Novel

Michael Cromwell

ISBN: Softcover   978-1-6698-6253-6
               eBook   978-1-6698-6254-3

Print information available on the last page.

Rev. date: 01/30/2023

To order additional copies of this book, contact:
Xlibris
844-714-8691
www.Xlibris.com
Orders@Xlibris.com
850256

Dedication:

This book is dedicated to my mother Joyce Ann Cromwell Dabit (1940-2011), who loved San Francisco, California, a beautiful but complicated city. I will see her in Heaven one day!

PROLOGUE

The conscience is a valuable tool for human beings, but even with it fully active, men do not always do good. Often the conscience is an afterthought or inconvenience, but fear is also an obstacle and so is pride, which tells the conscience that the individual is in charge of affairs and should not be challenged.

Around us are many who have been offered the choice of repentance and redemption in such matters, chosen such, and eternity has been granted theirs to enjoy and explore. But far more have rejected such opportunity, allowed pride to sear their consciences in life and are now only accessible through audible wails and gnashing teeth. Believe me, I know. I can hear them.

The creator gave men consciences for a reason: to follow and obey the laws that He created. One of them involves having compassion for fellow men and doing right by them, because if we do right by our fellow men, we show that we can do right by the creator. Though the creator does not have to be logical and can defy logic, that does make logical sense.

Take the case of **Grady Jonas,** who is now here with us. However, he almost did not make it. In his case, greed and pride combined to override his conscience, but suffering returned him to it. The key is that the conscience should be never too far from the surface; otherwise it may be unreachable and irretrievable, while the conscience should always be impervious to the cares of the human world. This last lesson proved to be Grady's greatest challenge.

CHAPTER I

Though Grady Jonas heard the trash trucks moving outside his window on a Monday morning in 1996, it was the war going on inside his apartment building that woke him. It was his neighbors again: the white woman across the hall, Lorraine, and the new Hispanic family that had recently moved directly above him. Lately, their feud had been irritating Grady more than normal. Most mornings recently, he heard the footsteps above his apartment and then came the clanging of the pots from across the hall. Usually Grady just turned on the TV and tuned out most of the racket, but this morning he was more perturbed than usual. As he flipped on the TV, he mumbled something under his breath in disgust.

Grady did not need the annoyance, especially this morning. He wasn't sure why this morning was any different. Perhaps it was the general malaise and dissatisfaction he was beginning to have with life, which he could not completely identify. Perhaps it was his age, perhaps it was his health, or perhaps it was his race. Perhaps it was that the world and people were changing in ways that he did not like and could not understand. Something was eating at him that was making him feel more unstable and desperate lately. Maybe it was just because it was a Monday.

In any case, he had to get ready for work. As he got up and walked around, the noise only irritated him further and he had to harden himself as he moved around his apartment. He picked up the bottle that was on the table in front of him. Looking at it only reminded him of the way he felt. He placed the bottle in a paint-chipped cabinet, knowing he would probably see it again later this evening after work.

In a moment, the movement in the apartment above suddenly turned into running sprints, like some kind of a gymnasium basketball drill. Grumbling again, Grady steeled himself to ignore it and headed for the bathroom. When he got there, he spat violently into the toilet, relieved his urine that had built up over night, and then brushed his teeth. He had to be at work at his office building in an hour and a half.

When he walked out of the bathroom, the trash truck noises had subsided, but those of his neighbors remained intermittent, mixed with the noise from one of the ubiquitous morning television shows.

Grady did not watch a lot of television, unless it was the local news. There seemed to be less and less on television that interested someone from his generation. In the evenings, he struggled to find something relevant to watch; but in the mornings, between the smiling faces, cooking segments, and celebrity interviews, he enjoyed hearing about the San Francisco Bay Area where he lived.

But as he watched the images on the machine and got ready for work, the raucousness around him seemed to increase in intensity. The Hispanic family upstairs was in a fight with Lorraine. The conflict was over morning noise, the same noise that Grady was hearing now. Their squabble had been going on for about three weeks and Grady had tried not to let it bother him.

The best he could tell was that Lorraine, who only worked occasionally and with whom he had been neighbors with for a while, resented the Hispanic father, mother, and three children moving into the apartment building several months ago. She had told Grady that she was bothered by the noise the family brought with it. He believed it was more than that. He believed she was prejudiced.

"They shoulda stayed where they belonged, in the Mission District," she told Grady about a week ago. "This area is gentrifyin'."

Grady was not sure what that meant. But he responded with a natural concern for equal opportunity for all.

"But this is the Tenderloin. Anybody can live here," he said. "Color don't matter when you poor. Does it? It shouldn't."

"Look around you, Jonas," Loretta countered abruptly as they had stood in their hallway. "This area's changin'. Rich people trying to take over all of San Francisco."

She was right. The area was changing. Grady saw the changes going on around him. He could not deny that. Rich young white people, for the most part, were popping up everywhere in the Tenderloin District. They brought smiles on their faces, and coffee cups and dogs on leashes, in an area historically known for crime, drug use and trafficking, prostitution, seedy hotels, and other types of shady living and lifestyles. Grady just figured that the rich white people were running out of room in other parts of the city.

But then again, he knew from growing up in the South almost 50 years earlier that white people usually moved where they wanted to and took what they wanted when they wanted it, often without asking. Next thing you knew, they just had it, and sometimes what they took was what you had. This was nothing new to him.

He had not bothered to ask more about Lorraine's specific problem with the Hispanic family. They were not rich, so what did their presence have to do with the "gentrifyin'?"

Nevertheless, what had resulted in recent weeks was a noise contest which Grady had to sit and experience firsthand. He felt caught in the middle but did not feel like getting involved. He had put up with a lot in life and he was not going to let a little noise get to him, especially when he considered it silly. So far, there had only been one outright confrontation, with the Hispanic father complaining about Lorraine's banging on her ceiling. Since then, there had only been noise, but nothing Grady could not handle.

In the Tenderloin, as with life in general, one had to know when to mind one's business and Grady was good at minding his. Between his early days in the racist South and his latter days in the wild and wacky West, life had instructed him to put up with a lot. Getting too involved could lead to unneeded frustration and problems, or worse.

Continuing to ignore the noises but still annoyed with them, he opened his window for a little air and peace of mind before he would finish getting ready for work. It was 7 am now; he had to be there at 8. His window opened to a fire escape landing and looked down into an alley. He was on the second floor. He walked to work and to get to his building on time, he would have to leave precisely at 7:30 am. Over the years, he had honed the morning walk down to specific timing. Catching all the lights and maneuvering through the capricious downtown San

Francisco intersections and tourist traffic, he could be at his building usually by 7:58 am.

As he opened the window, he let in the early morning sounds and smells of the city. San Francisco, for good or ill, was now inside his apartment. Unbeknownst to Grady, the window acted as a portal through which the seductive city exacted its influence. That morning, opening the window gave Grady feelings of physical regeneration and grandiosity. He was grateful for this because he needed relief from his hangover and a brief retreat from his neighbors.

Grady climbed out onto the fire escape. He could not see much because his view across the alley met the brick wall of an opposing Tenderloin apartment building. But it was the San Francisco air that he wanted most.

Despite the alley smells that came with it, the brisk San Francisco air had always been an elixir like no other he had ever experienced before arriving in the city. It seemed to have a lifeforce of its own and it had played no small part in he and his wife's decision to remain in the city when they arrived from Georgia some forty years earlier.

Grady knew that there was something unusual about the air, just like the city itself and its inhabitants. The San Francisco air got a hold on you once you were there and it took a particular kind of strength to resist and escape it. It was charming and inviting, tempting and seductive. It still had a hold on Grady after all these years. In general, there was something about living in San Francisco that made one feel important and privileged, regardless of ethnic background, or economic status.

Grady needed the air. A few deep breaths of the San Francisco air were necessary for him to feel better, but he stayed outside for only about five minutes. He had to get to work.

Before going inside though, along with taking in the garbage smells from the alley below, he could also hear the sounds of the rising city: the car motors, the sighing of public buses as they braked and lurched through the downtown streets, the odd shout from an early morning business or deliveryman, or the berserk cry of one of the often mad homeless who had either just woken up or had stayed up all night. As usual, the sounds and smells could be both pleasant and disturbing.

After letting the San Francisco air envelope his entire 65-year-old body, Grady ducked back inside his apartment to finish getting ready for work. Almost immediately though, he was assaulted again by the sounds of the early morning duel between neighbors, which seemed to have escalated even more in his brief absence. To shut them out and get ready for work, Grady turned up the television a little louder.

Before he went to work, he wanted to hear more anyway about a news story he had been following, about a young black man from across the bay in Oakland who had been shot. The man and some of his friends had been out late and got into a fight with another group of young men. When the police came, they separated everyone and there was a lot of yelling and screaming. Amid all the confusion, a white police officer had shot one of the young black men in the back.

This was the biggest story in the entire Bay Area at the time, and since it reminded Grady of the days when he was growing up as a boy in Macon, Georgia, he found himself interested in the outcome.

He mumbled, "They just killed that boy, just like that. That was just like a lynchin'. If they can get away with that, they can get away with anything."

The sights and sounds of social injustice only added to the other frustrations which had been building in him lately, but he tried to calm himself. Even still, the story would probably play again before he went to work, and he knew he would watch since the images and emotions of his youthful days in the South had never completely exited his consciousness. Meanwhile, he went through his routine: a shower, shave, and the putting on of his uniform. To completely rid himself of his mild hangover, he also would get a cup of coffee when he got to work, though he generally did not drink much coffee and it was never more than one cup a day.

Deciding that he would eat something quickly before leaving, he moved to his kitchen cabinet to get his cooking materials. But then, the banging from across the hall sounded off again. This was followed by a rush of footsteps coming down the stairs at the end of the hall.

It's the Hispanic father again, Grady thought. He had something to say and Grady could not resist visiting his door to see the upcoming altercation, even though it might make him late for work. He cracked the door open and looked down the hall to the right.

Outside Lorraine's door, he saw the Hispanic father. He had dark hair and a mustache. He was short in stature, and he was shirtless. A boy about three quarters his size was standing next to him. The man and his wife had two boys and a girl from what Grady had been able to gather so far. The two largest apartments in the building were on the third floor and the Hispanic family occupied one.

"¡*No mas señora*!" the man said. "Or I will call the manager."

"Call him if you want," came a defiant shriek from inside Lorraine's apartment.

"*¡No mas!*" the man said again. "We live here also, *tambien*."

"Get away from my door or I'll call the manager myself, you hear me?" came another throaty threat from behind Lorraine's closed door.

Frustrated because he could not get to Lorraine face-to-face, or because he could not understand or gauge her intentions, the man abruptly pivoted to return to his apartment. His son, who had said nothing, followed behind obediently.

"I ain't never going to get another quiet morning," Grady mumbled to himself as he closed his door. "Both of them fools," he added. As he walked back into his apartment, he realized that he was disappointed by the limited activity. He had wanted to see a full out conflict, and this thought made him laugh silently to himself. It was the closest thing to self-generated laughter he had experienced in a long time.

Within the next half hour, Grady had fixed breakfast and stood dressed in his blue blazer, gray slacks, white shirt, and a red tie. He was ready for work. Before he left, however, he did manage to catch a news update, which said that the officer who had shot the young black man in the back had not been arrested, but was on paid leave from his department.

Grady was frustrated and disappointed by this turn of events. Murder, public murder, is what Grady thought, just like Willie Boyd back in Macon in '48. He had been one of the only people who saw Willie hanging from the tree and the incident had propelled him toward leaving the South for good.

Back in the South during those times, there were no protests like the one he saw now on the TV. If there had been, there might have been more lynchings, and more deaths. Black people had not gotten *tough enough* at that point. There was not a whole lot they would do. But as he was watching through the TV, he saw black people in Oakland, protesting the decision regarding the officer, yelling and screaming all kinds of reactions and attitudes, and none of them were in favor of the police.

"Eye for an eye!" he heard from one protester.

"What do we got to do to be free and equal in this country!?" he heard from another, who had taken the microphone from the TV reporter.

In the brief TV segment, there was one protester who stood out to Grady in particular. He was short in stature and wore dark sunglasses and a red beret. He looked like one of those crazy blacks from the 1960s that Grady could never really follow or completely understand. He stood out, not only for his apparent youth and his calm demeanor, but because Grady could not see his eyes to get a complete sense of him. There was something both dangerous and ominous that came across about him.

"Time gon' come," the young man said, attempting to sound prophetic. "Time's comin'. This a war and not a battle. Our historical oppressors gon' git theirs one day. It ain't over yet. Far from it. Their time gonna come and our time gonna come too," he finished cryptically, and his words were met with a small cheer from the crowd of other, mostly young, Oakland blacks. The TV reporter, a young white woman, was jostled by the crowd, but still managed to smile brightly and energetically, as the cheer rose up around her. She seemed happy to be there.

Grady also felt partially inspired by the young man's words and the call for justice and revenge. At least someone was saying something, and things were not getting swept under the rug.

But he had to leave for work. He would keep an eye on the Oakland situation to see what happened next.

Before leaving he made sure to close his window. The San Francisco air would not be allowed inside his apartment while he was away, and he was careful not to give intruders access to his apartment from the fire escape.

"Lookin' sharp Jonas," Lorraine said as he exited his apartment into the hallway. She was hanging outside her door as Grady tried to leave. Her apartment was a few feet down, on the other side of the hall. Grady had lived in the building five years and Lorraine about seven. By Tenderloin District standards, their tenure in the building had been long, and aside from Spike, the former Hell's Angel who lived on the first floor, Grady and Lorraine were the longest tenured tenants in the building. Other people on the floor came and went. That was the nature of the Tenderloin.

"Runnin' late," he responded briskly, and he might be late if he did not leave immediately. He had no time to talk to Lorraine, though they did talk once in a while. It was obvious to him that she was in a combative early morning mood anyway and if he let her, she would interfere with his schedule.

"Did I make too much noise this morning?" she asked. "It wasn't my fault you know."

Grady looked at her sideways. She was leaning against the inside of her doorway trying to look sexy. He had had his share of women in life, even white women on a couple of occasions, and he knew the look. But he had to keep moving. He had rarely been late to work in the seven years he had worked for his company.

"Not too much for me. I'm used to it by now," he said, to which Lorraine responded with a self-amused cackle of sorts. The laugh revealed a few missing teeth as she brushed back her uncombed, morning hair. She wore a loose-fitting white t-shirt and jeans and was about 10 years younger than Grady.

"Ok baby, you have a good day," she said.

"Yea, I'll talk to you later," he said, happy to avoid an extended conversation, about anything right now.

He took his building's stairs to get to the first floor and exit. Before leaving the building, he heard hard and loud rock music coming from Spike's apartment. The music, as usual, sounded like chaos and destruction, or the end of the world. He had also learned to ignore this, to harden himself to Tenderloin influences in general.

Now with the building behind him, Lorraine's laugh, Spike's music, and the Hispanic family's morning footsteps exorcised from his mind for the moment, he took his place on the sidewalk with the rest of humanity. For the most part, he was still content to be part of it. He liked his job and he liked San Francisco, even though he was becoming grouchier and more unsettled lately in general.

San Francisco was good to those who adored it and repelled those who did not. For now, Grady resided on the positive side of this charming, though bawdy, lewd, and sometimes rude environment, which was often, and for various reasons, equated with being one of the most wicked and sinful cities in the world.

CHAPTER II

As Grady walked down the San Francisco sidewalk, he passed numerous coffee and bagel shops, newsstands, and hotel fronts, some with ornately dressed doormen. Around him, taxis, buses, tourists, and workers prepared for their day.

He felt invigorated again. Whatever had happened earlier was now behind him, and that was part of San Francisco's charm. It could pull you out of the doldrums by stimulating your senses in various pleasant and positive ways, realigning your thinking and attitude. Rarely did one worry about what the city would ask in return.

It was the beginning of a northern California spring, meanwhile. The winter rains had passed, and March brought in cool, breezy temperatures and blazing sunlight, which fired through the puffy clouds in the sky. This atmosphere could make anyone feel good to be alive, and the early morning tourists that Grady passed on his way to work showed this on their hungry, beaming faces.

Many had never seen or felt anything quite like San Francisco before and sometimes seeing their reactions made Grady feel proud that he still called the city home. San Franciscans knew San Francisco, all flaws aside, and that was the only thing that mattered, as far as they were concerned. Later the fog might roll in off the bay and create a completely different mood in the city; but the idea was to glean as much as possible from the day that the city was about to present.

Unlike some of the other guards where Grady worked, Grady walked to work in his uniform. For Grady, it was not just that he still had a job at his age, but also that he could walk to his job in his blue crested blazer and gray slacks for all the world to see.

He still looked good despite his age, and because he looked good, he felt as important as anyone else that came across his path. Though he worked as a $12-an-hour security guard, he took pride in striding down Sutter Street, past fashionable Union Square, through key parts of San Francisco's downtown, to Montgomery Street and the heart of the West Coast's financial district, where his building was located. In self-generating dignity and carriage, he was like some genteel figure of days gone by, his large, handsome head held high, and his strides measured.

Despite his confidence on these walks, he was becoming a dwindling minority in a city of minorities. San Francisco had never been known for having a large black population and the ones that were there were either ultra-successful or lived in abject poverty and homelessness. There were simply not as many blacks on the West Coast as there were on the East and in the South, whereas the Hispanics and Asians came easily and regularly from Mexico, Central America, and the Pacific Rim nations respectively.

California was never really a great Mecca for blacks in general. The black population that had existed when Grady moved to the city in 1951 had dwindled over the years. There was a time when Grady remembered seeing many more black faces in the downtown area, but they had vanished. On some mornings his was the only black face in sight. But Grady still trusted San Francisco.

For him, the city itself trumped any negative trends or attitudes that he was aware of at any time. So, if other blacks had chosen to move away, then that was their problem. The city laid down the rules for Grady, and he still liked following them. In the end, San Francisco took care of its own: those who chose to love it back.

Sometimes people would stare at Grady, in his suit, tie, gray slacks, and with his caramel-colored skin, but he would just ignore them. San Francisco had made him, as it made others who called it home, a bit arrogant. So, for those who stared at him, he merely cast them off as "ignorant tourists."

Most of the other blacks that did still work in the city were security guards like Grady, bus and railcar drivers, and BART operators. A lot of them did not live in the city because they could not afford the high rent prices, and property values. Some lived as far as away as Sacramento. Many from the much larger Mexican population did these same kinds of jobs. They also cleaned office buildings in great numbers, after the mostly white and Asian workers went home for the day. This was the case in Grady's own building, each and every night.

Grady tried not to see the world in terms of color, though it was becoming more of a struggle as time passed. San Francisco had taught him not to be racist. To a large extent, the city had softened the hardness planted in him during his early years in the Deep South, though he was not completely naïve. He knew there were still great inequities in life, economically if nothing else. At least San Francisco seemed to try to mitigate these problems, in its own ways.

Across the Bay, where many more blacks lived, Oakland was a different city, and its problems were unique to it. Some of those problems had prevented Grady from ever considering a move there, and Oakland also had more crime. San Francisco at least maintained a spirit of trying to work out social problems to everyone's benefit. So, it was better just to stay. In Grady's mind, there was something inarticulate and inaudible that spoke to him through the San Francisco air, almost like a subtle serpent would speak, saying, "This is the natural order of life. Be content and fill your role and you will be protected and satisfied."

While walking to work, Grady still felt happy and content, though he was not looking forward to the meeting with his building's new owners.

Grady's building was on Montgomery Street. It was about eight blocks from his apartment and it was a 48-story skyscraper, one of the tallest in the city. It was not *the* tallest building, but on clear days from the higher floors, one got panoramic views of many parts of the ultra-scenic San Francisco Bay Area. Grady had been to all the floors and had seen the streets of San Francisco from many angles. He had even been on the roof on several occasions. He went up there once during a thick fog, where he could not see anything. It was as if he had gotten off an elevator and walked directly into a cloud.

"This might be as close to Heaven as I'm gon' git," he had joked to himself on that occasion. He had gone up to the roof to inspect it, but was unable to because of the fog. His visit into the middle of a cloud that day had been brief.

After navigating early morning crowds and traffic, he arrived at his building one minute late. He relieved the overnight guard and then waited for Buddy, the young white kid he had been working with lately.

Buddy was new to San Francisco. He dressed like a punk rocker and was from somewhere back on the East Coast, like Delaware, Maryland, or New Jersey, or someplace like that. Grady really didn't care which one and could not remember. All Grady could remember about him at any given time were his poor work habits: coming in late, being away from his post, flirting with women, and generally being unprofessional. Perhaps the new management coming in would set him straight, as the previous one had not. Buddy got away with a lot, as far as Grady was concerned.

When Grady arrived, Buddy was nowhere to be seen and Grady mumbled something negative under his breath as he got himself organized behind the guard desk in his building's ornate, golden lobby. Two guards worked both of the day shifts and one worked the graveyard shift. These days, he and Buddy usually worked the morning shift together.

In general, Buddy was one of those starry-eyed newcomers to San Francisco. Like most, he had been immediately seduced by the city's lax morality and civic permissiveness. One could get away with much in San Francisco, publicly and privately. Many people, especially the young, took great advantage of these concessions. Grady tried to be patient when dealing with Buddy as a worker, though sometimes Buddy could push the limit.

Placing himself in position behind the desk under the lobby's high and cavernous white and beige ceiling, Grady took his post. While early morning tenants, visitors, and delivery people entered and exited the lobby, Grady checked the security monitors. He also tried to greet some of the people he knew. Soon enough, Grady caught a quick view of Buddy through the camera that surveyed the food court area downstairs. He had a cup of coffee in his hand and was walking with Big Eric, the head janitor. They appeared to be heading to the elevator on their way up to the lobby.

"Thas it...!" Grady said to himself in disgust. "Thas enough!" he added, as he considered again that Buddy had little regard for manning his post, and therefore, for the job in general. They were supposed to post behind the desk at precisely 8 am to go over the night shift reports. The desk was never to be left unattended.

But while he waited for his partner to reach the desk, Grady did his job. He continued to greet the early morning tenants and surveyed the video monitors to make sure everything was in order. Some people coming through the lobby would greet him "hello" in the morning, but most would not. They were rushing to and fro, up and down, back and forth, carrying coffee, briefcases and purses, and various handheld breakfasts. Most visitors and tenants in the building were white and Asian.

"I know what you're gonna say. My bad," Buddy said, apologizing his way around the corner from downstairs. "But a tenant wanted me to open up a ET closet downstairs and I had to score some coffee on the way back upstairs. It's all good!"

Grady only looked at Eric and the two black men mused over the latest antics and excuses of the brash white kid from the East Coast. Grady in particular wondered if either black man would be allowed to work the front desk, or work in the building at all, if they modified the English language the way that Buddy did.

Meanwhile, Buddy's blond hair was coated in gel, as usual, and slicked back. Their boss, Tony, had ordered him to tone down the spiky, punk-style he sported when he first arrived three months ago. But he had managed to keep one of the two earrings he had, and he still had a red and black flame tattoo that shone on the side of his neck, which was easily visible to building tenants and visitors. How he had gotten hired with the way he looked was still a mystery to Grady, who always tried to maintain a professional and dignified bearing.

Unlike Grady, who wore his uniform to work, Buddy always came to work in jeans, and with his uniform in a backpack. Early on, his uniform had been in awful shape when he put it on, with wrinkles and stains, which had precipitated Tony's first "negotiation" with management over Buddy. It had come up that though he had gotten the job, Buddy was living in flop houses and was even homeless on occasion. Therefore, management decided to accommodate him as best it could, even allowing him into the company office to iron his uniform and get better groomed before work in the morning. Both Grady and Tony, who was the senior guard and who was also black, had marveled at such treatment, wondering if either of them would be extended the same courtesies by their employer if they faced similar circumstances.

Despite such treatment from management, Buddy remained on Tony's short list, reserved for those who could be fired at any moment. Tony had been in the army and did not tolerate too much disorder. For Tony, Buddy was still too informal and unprofessional with tenants and visitors and his appearance was still substandard. But Tony was the boss of the guards and not the boss of the building and could only do so much. Grady liked Buddy personally, even though he still got under Grady's skin professionally. Grady was mostly afraid that the young man's slack approach to work could make a co-worker look bad. So, Grady always kept a close eye on Buddy as well. Grady had grown up with some standards to live by, though he felt that such standards were now lost on the younger generation.

⌒✶⌒

For the rest of the morning it was a typical Monday, with the same kinds of activities probably being conducted in other, similar office buildings throughout downtown San Francisco. There were other security guards like Grady greeting visitors, helping people to find information and locate clients, and generally trying to provide disciplined and professional faces for their buildings. Occasionally there might be some excitement, where somebody would get into a building without security knowing about it. Maybe some vagrant, of which San Francisco possessed many, would start up something out on the sidewalk and one of the guards would have to go outside to reason with the individual and try to get him or her to move along and out of trouble.

There was nothing that dramatic this particular morning. Grady only wanted to make it through the day. His head still wrung a little from last night. He hoped the meeting this afternoon with "the new team" would go smoothly, so he could make it home peacefully at the end of the day.

⌒✶⌒

That meeting, with the new building owners called New Vision Properties, eventually rolled around at 1 pm. Buddy went to the meeting with Grady while a guard from the business office watched the desk. Buddy and Grady took the elevator up together to the 38th floor.

"You ready for the new owners?" Grady asked, just to get an idea what the wily young man might be thinking, and to compare that thinking to his own.

"I can take 'em or leave 'em," Buddy responded apathetically while smoothing his hair in the reflective elevator door. "As long as I gets paid. Know what I mean? That's the bottom line." He shrugged, putting his comb back in this pocket, and added, "It's all about the money, pops. That's the bottom line. It ain't about who likes you or respects you. They livin' large and we ain't. We don't mean jack to any of 'em. They gonna be the same as the last bunch."

Grady was a little surprised at Buddy's response, considering how much the current company had done to make sure the kid stayed employed.

"You might have a point," Grady said. "But only time'll tell. Meanwhile, you should try to treat people with respect, and respect what you have. That's what a lot of you young people need to learn. Right?"

"Aright pops," Buddy said, nonchalantly, as they were about to reach their floor. "I heard it before. Lectures like that is one reason why I left home," he added and chuckled to himself as they exited the elevator.

The meeting was supposed to be about 20 minutes to a half hour, just long enough to introduce the guards to the new owners. But while Grady was there, one of the new people asked him to go all the way down the basement to retrieve a card table that would be needed for activities later in the day.

While Grady did this without complaint, he found that he did not like the tone of the man who had asked him to complete the task. It had sounded like an order, and the man had not asked the obviously more junior guard, Buddy. The tone of the man who had asked Grady to get the table was reminiscent of those of white men during Grady's early years in the South. Grady made a mental note of this man's particular attitude, while everyone else seemed reasonably pleasant.

When he came back up from getting the table, Grady ate a donut amidst shaking hands with the very young-looking management team. Buddy flirted with one of the office assistants, an Asian girl with long black hair that reached all the way down to her waist. She and everyone else seemed no older than 35, unlike the old owners at Hallmark Properties, who had maintained the building since Grady first arrived.

Those owners, and some staff, were closer to Grady's age and he had a relationship with some of them. Grady had noticed that everything was geared toward the young these days and he had not been surprised by the age of people from the new management team he and Buddy met.

After the meeting, Grady took his daily walk to patrol the perimeter of the building. This took about 20 minutes. He had to choose between leaving Buddy behind the desk and letting him patrol the building. He often chose to patrol himself because Buddy could sometimes get in more trouble if out in the public. Grady was glad that he had chosen the patrol today because the city's atmosphere felt like the old days when he had first started working at the building.

Outside, the climate and vibe of the city were exquisite. Despite its problems, San Francisco had radiance and a charm unique among American cities. Today, there was a mix of warm temperatures, clear skies, and light breezes to boost the spirits and make one feel vital, relevant, and connected to something greater than one's self.

Looking around the streets, Grady thought everyone looked happy. It was the San Francisco of the old days, and Grady soaked it all in, taking an extra few minutes on his patrol to get the most out of the day's feeling. He saw the punk bike messengers gabbing on Sansome Street, and the tourists with eyes glowing over the wonder of downtown San Francisco.

Downtown was a kaleidoscope of images, some lovely enough to dazzle, and some gross enough to repel. However, San Francisco's rich natural beauty always seemed to overwhelm and overpower its penchants for occasional human ugliness. Today, that beauty cast Grady in an old spell and he felt buoyed enough to believe that his life might begin to take a turn for the better and away from the sour, foul moods he had been experiencing lately.

CHAPTER III

Grady's reverent nostalgia for the city would be short-lived, however, as when he reentered the building from the street, Buddy was again, nowhere in sight. The guard desk was unmanned, and there was a large group of people lingering near it, appearing to be in search of help. Grady quickly used his walkie-talkie to try to radio Buddy, but he received no response to this.

"Hello," a white man in his 30s said.

Grady assumed his position behind the desk, silently simmering over Buddy's absence. "May I help you sir?" Grady said after gathering himself.

"Name's Mike Coverdale. I'm here to see my brother. He works in the building. He's a lawyer. But we're not sure what floor he's on. His last name is Coverdale too. He belongs to the firm of Settle, Pilgrim, and Gentile. He told us the building number and its location, but we don't recall the floor number. Can you help us please?"

"Yes sir, jes give me a minute or two," Grady responded after taking in the size of the man's entourage. Around him were about 20 people, a sea of white faces, young and old. It was an incredibly large group for any time of day, and there to see only one person. Grady had, in fact, never seen such a large, unified group in the lobby.

They were all well-dressed, clean cut, and maybe from apparent wealth, though they did not look to be from the city, or even from California. He could have directed them all to the building menu board behind them, but it was being redesigned at the moment. All queries, therefore, had to go through the lobby desk.

The group of people in front of him also looked strong and hearty; they were not quite western, but perhaps from somewhere in the Midwest. There were children among them, with bright, healthy faces. There were women, mostly around the age of the speaker, several teenage boys and girls and there was one old woman who stood right at the counter.

She appeared to be some kind of matriarch to the clan. She was small-framed, but stood out nonetheless. This old white woman, who might have been in her 80s, seemed to eye Grady more closely than the others. In fact, there was a kind of fondness in her eyes for him, but it was a peculiar kind of fondness to Grady. It was a look he had seen before, somewhere in past perhaps, but he could not place it right now. At the moment for Grady, there was also a look in her filmy blue eyes of a kind of child-like instability, or even lunacy.

Dismissing them all for the sake of performing his job, Grady began his search of the building computer database to locate the firm the man had mentioned. He had heard of it before, but could not recall the floor exactly.

Buddy was still away, meanwhile, and though it was close to the end of their eight-to-four shift, even more people had trickled through the lobby doors and up to the counter looking for information.

Grady had not expected such an onslaught near the end of his shift, nor was he expecting to have to handle it alone. Had Buddy merely left for the day early, without giving notice? Maybe he had simply quit? Grady would put neither past him.

The large group in front of him seemed to be drawing the attention of other lobby occupants and passersby in general. After a few minutes, as Grady tried to serve them all, sweat started to form on his forehead, which those awaiting his service started to notice. The problem was that the computer was moving slowly, taking time to download the building's tenant directory, making everyone wait.

"We havin' some trouble with the computer right now," he said, looking up to everyone. "Jes give it a minute please."

None of them seemed to be in a big hurry and they seemed content to wait. Grady was not really in a big hurry either, but also being perturbed about Buddy's absence, made him appear anxious overall.

With a lull in the action as they all waited for the technology to operate properly, the old woman in front of him began to eye him more intently, and Grady felt the need to look into the woman's controlling eyes, to respond to some inquiry that she was either unwilling or unable to utter. He had to look *down* at her as she was no more than five feet in height compared to his frame, which was slightly over six feet.

Despite her size though, her staring began to make him feel uncomfortable, as if he had no essence, or that she was trying to temporarily bind that essence in some way; and even before she ever even opened her mouth, he knew that she was preparing to say something. Somehow, he was going to be punished for showing her any kind of specific attention at all. He had shown a kind of weakness that everyone within hearing distance would soon regret.

"You're a good nigger," the old woman said, through a voice that was stinging, but meant to encourage at the same time. "You're trying to do the best you can and we appreciate that. We need more niggers like you in this mixed up world."

"Grandmother!!!" came a shriek from the man named Coverdale. The kids, who stood next to their great-grandmother, said nothing, maintaining their playful, childish appearances. Two young women near the front went quickly from looking at the old woman in shock, to looking at Grady to observe his reaction, one averting her eyes from him quickly after doing so.

After a few moments, Michael Coverdale spoke: "I'd like to apologize, she doesn't get out much. She has Alzheimer's too. We're from Kentucky. We're here to see my brother, her grandson. He just got a job at this firm and we're here to help him celebrate later today."

Grady said nothing at first but bent his head down to keep looking at the screen before him. San Francisco had enough craziness. This was nothing new. In some ways, this was minor compared to the things he experienced in the city on a daily basis.

He had been called a "nigger" before also many times, when race relations were much worse than they were now. He had even been called the word a few times since moving out West. So he was generally unfazed at the moment. He just wanted to do his job and get the people out of the lobby and on their way.

But with the slow computer inadvertently forcing him to remember earlier times, he quickly assessed that this old woman must be from an earlier generation and that her mind was somehow still caught up in it.

"Doncha' worry about it sir," Grady told Mike Coverdale through a stony, business-only face. Then he joked, "I been called worse than that over the years. Now let's see if we can get ya'll on your way, all right?" he added.

Buddy's whereabouts entered his mind again and that became a real source of anger. Buddy, ironically, might be able to help now. Where was he?

Michael Coverdale responded with a relieved smile of his own, only to be followed by his grandmother, whose mind had not calculated or even acknowledged any of the previous dialogue.

"My husband always said the only good nigger was a dead nigger," she added matter-of-factly, "but I never believed that myself." Her eyes, which were now locked on Grady again, now seemed to have gone from deep blue to purple. "I always believed…" she tried to continue, but she was quickly stopped short in one motion by her grandson's hand, which was slapped across her mouth like a large baseball mitt.

Lydia Coverdale quickly found herself urgently, but gently, being ushered away from the counter to an area of soft, lobby sofas, with her grandson's full palm still around her mouth. The young man looked like he might have tied his grandmother up with rope if he could have, and other people, particularly those *entering* the lobby from the street, could not help but notice the unusual activity between the young man and old woman.

For the first time, the rest of the large group recognized that something was going on and began to stir near the rear. The women in the front and the children looked over at their grandmother in wonderment. Grady stood there urging the computer with useless, repetitive keystrokes. Looking over at the grandson and the old woman, he began to feel wounded by the whole incident for the first time.

"I'd like to apologize again," one of the women near the front said. "He's my husband and she's my in-law. We have trouble with her from time to time. She suffers from a few things, not the least of which is Alzheimer's disease. Because she's a part of the family, we wanted her to see her grandson in his new office. But again, I would like to apologize to you for all of us." With curly, auburn hair that bounced above her robust and freckled face, this woman seemed very sincere to Grady.

"Not ta worry," Grady said briskly, trying to be polite—one of the prime requirements of his job. "I done seen it all over the years." Secretly though, he just wanted them all out of the lobby and out of his life. He wanted the computer to reveal their floor, and quickly.

Looking down into the computer screen, he saw that the letters had gone past "S" and were now at "V." Scrolling up with a few button taps, he found "Settle," and firmly called out, "Settle, Pilgrim, and Gentile, 15th Floor." He then quickly looked away to the interests of others who had trickled up the counter and checked the video monitors for the whereabouts of Buddy.

The great group filed into the elevator banks, seeming to huddle together for greater anonymity, an aura of shame speaking through their movements as word of what had happened had apparently spread throughout the entire group.

Michael Coverdale sent his grandmother up with the large group, himself staying behind to have one final word with Grady. Ironically, Buddy walked up at the same time, just before their shift was to end.

"I'd like to apologize again, man," Coverdale said. "She's 90-years-old," he added, smiling. "Can you believe that? Ninety-years-old," he added for emphasis. "It's amazing that she can still think at all. I hope I live to be that old."

Still smiling, hoping that his face might weaken whatever resentment might have welled up in Grady, Coverdale concluded, "I'd just like to repeat again that we are really sorry. We're really not prejudiced, if that's what you're thinking, but people from that generation…well you know how that goes. You remember some of that stuff back then, right?"

Buddy, now behind the desk and appearing to do his job, occasionally looked over to see what Grady and the stranger were discussing.

"I remember that time very well, young man," Grady uttered through a newly sonorous tone, almost as if he had many stories to tell. "What do you know about it?"

Feeling an upcoming challenge that he had not anticipated, Michael Coverdale tried to muster up a combination of confidence and delicate politeness, and hurriedly so, because he wanted to join his family.

"Well, I am not an expert on those times, sir," he said, "but I know they were rough for a lot of people, especially for your people." He was neither smiling nor frowning now. His countenance was just flat with a newfound kind of resolve, as if he were now in a fight or competition of sorts.

"Those times were hard," Grady said, suddenly not wanting to let the young man get away without some lesson learned. "But forget about it. Times are better now. This a different world now than it used to be. Go on and catch up with your family now and have a nice day."

"Ok, thanks man. Have a nice day too, and sorry again," Coverdale said before briskly walking off to catch the next elevator.

"Boy, what are you doing? Where you been?" Grady said roughly, after turning to Buddy. Part of him wanted to blame Buddy for all that had just happened. "That's the main question. I'm not gonna take much more of this. You lucky Tony ain't here."

"I was talking to that woman from the 29th floor and I lost track of time. I apologize and I promise it won't happen again," he said, trying to muster some humility. "It was close to the end of the shift and I thought you would be right back."

"You playin' with fire boy," Grady said, now standing next to Buddy so that they were both facing the lobby, and those who came and went. "You always playin' with fire, but you ain't really got burnt yet. The new owners might not put up with it. Even if I'm not watchin' you, somebody else always is."

"Won't happen again. I promise this time," was Buddy's response. Buddy had wanted to ask what had transpired while he was away, but he decided against it. Instead, like Grady, he was ready to leave for the day. He planned on getting a new tattoo after work. "Where's that fat Russian?" he said.

Within minutes, the old Russian guard, Marko, was strolling into the lobby. He was always on time and, like Grady, wore his uniform to work. He only used the dressing room to put on his tie. He had gray hair with a receding, comb-over hairline, a pot belly, and he waddled a little when he walked. But he was a responsible guard and, like Grady, took his job seriously.

"There's that fat Ruskie," Buddy said without missing a beat. "I'll see you tomorrow. But I forgot to tell you. They want to know if you can work the swing tomorrow instead. That other guy can't make it. I told them I couldn't. But I told them I would ask you. I would if I could though, but I'm going to hang out at the beach with some people."

"Go home boy," Grady said, tired of listening to Buddy at this point. He would call management upstairs and tell them it would be ok. He had started out working swing shift before moving to mornings. It meant that he could sleep in a little later, get off later at night, and they would probably give him the day off in between, to recover so that he could return to mornings on Thursday.

Once Marko was ready to relieve him, Grady left for the day. As he walked home, the events of the day crept back into his head. What had happened with the old woman still irked him for sure, but he found himself just as irked by Buddy's behavior. The incident with the white man at the new management company even crept through his head. All these events were competing for space in his mind as he walked.

It seemed that such conflicts were becoming more prevalent in his daily life and he considered that because of them, the day had not been a good one. Each was an example of white people acting silly and crazy, in his opinion, though he had long ago learned to dismiss long meditations on their behaviors. He had trained himself to deal with white people and their behaviors when they came, and to defend himself when threatened by them. Neither episode today had reached the level where he actually felt threatened.

By the time he had reached his apartment, he had forgotten all about the previous events. The San Francisco air had done its magic again. It could be both tonic and instigator.

His building was quiet, though the afternoon streets were as charged up as usual. People, buses, tourists, and merchants moved about in every direction, trying not to run into each another. The Tenderloin District was the lower-class cousin of the wealthy Financial District where he worked, and he had learned to put up with the variety of noises, faces, and behaviors that could be found in the area. These elements made his environment colorful and interesting for him, and his neighborhood's impoverished humility provided a solid balance to the general arrogance of the place where he worked.

Inside his building, there was no sign of Lorraine or the other tenants. There had only been the dimming light bulb in the hallway that seemed to flicker now. Grady always noticed it before because it illuminated the path to his apartment. Once it went out, there would be complete darkness in that part of the hallway and neither Grady nor Lorraine wanted to buy a new bulb, insisting that management get a new one instead. The man who took care of those things, McTeague, was not always around when needed. Grady might have to up and buy a bulb, but he was still trying to avoid it. Let the bulb go out completely, and he would think about replacing it.

McTeague was usually around on Saturday mornings and Grady would try to corner him about the bulb then. Right now, the bulb had settled into a steady flicker.

Inside his apartment, Grady opened the window, his portal to the city, to let in the fresh air. The air this evening felt even better, as he anticipated sleeping in late the next morning. On the evening news, which he usually relaxed with, there was another story about the young Oakland man who had been shot by the police officer. They now revealed his name to be Arthur Grant. More and more it looked like the young man had been executed, shot in the back as he lay on the ground handcuffed and unarmed. Lawyers were now involved.

A gust of foul-smelling air entered Grady's apartment through the open window and he mumbled to himself in disgust as he ate a sandwich and watched the TV. He had learned to live with the San Francisco smells, which occasionally emanated from his alley.

The Oakland story seemed to use footage from its earlier broadcast. Grady again saw the strange but articulate militant black youth he saw in the morning. This time Grady found himself interested in what else the mysterious little radical might have to say. This young man was at least talking about fighting back, but in a calm, measured way. He said the same thing he had said in the morning, but Grady felt strangely empowered by the young man's words this time.

The TV news continued with more rising tensions in the Middle East and problems in other parts of the world also. Reported scandals had everyone pointing fingers at everyone else and folks on different channels were arguing heatedly about different issues. With every new image, Grady thought that the tone through the T.V. screen was palpable and he thought that the world was becoming more combative in general.

It was a complete reversal of the previous generation's Summer of Love. A kind of rage was not just outside his window, but it was everywhere it seemed, like some foul spirit from below sent to choke the life out of the masses of the surface world.

"I ain't crazy," he mumbled to himself, watching the different sides of the world through his TV set. "This world is crazy.

Gettin' crazier, every day. A little bit more every day. I ain't gonna let it make me crazy."

He got up and got his bottle from the cabinet. Sitting back on his couch, he muttered again, after taking a drink: "It's a cold world out there. I guess I have to be just like 'em. Kill or be killed; lie or be lied on; be weak or be strong." In general, there was a sense in the old man that the world was coming up behind him, eating at his heels and that he would have to find some way to beat it back or he might be completely engulfed or devoured by it.

He took another drink and then he heard some commotion outside his door. It was Lorraine. She was shouting angry inaudible comments in the hallway.

Tired, Grady ignored her and closed his eyes to sleep. Images of hate still emanated from the television's glowing blue screen. The air coming through his window smelled of decay.

CHAPTER IV

The next morning, after an uneventful night, he woke up refreshed. For the most part he had forgotten the events of the previous day. He had learned a while ago that he did not like letting negative thoughts linger in his mind. This was part of aging and maturity. After all, he had his own real-world issues to deal with, like physical survival, rent, food, and keeping a job. Grady understood that it would do no good to gripe, especially over the activities of an old white woman who was mentally unstable, and a silly-minded white kid who would be fired one day soon anyway.

The "free" morning passed surprisingly quickly and, before he knew it, it was time to go back to work and the swing shift. There had been no bickering between neighbors this morning to disturb him, so he felt generally well-rested. A little coffee, as it usually did, eliminated any semblance of a hangover.

He might see Buddy during the changeover between shifts—if the young man hung around long enough—but Grady would be working with Marko this evening. Grady had not yet decided whether to give a fresh report about Buddy's work habits to management. He might tell Tony first and let him handle it. The thought of a potential confrontation between those two gave Grady a twinge of pleasure and excitement as he walked to work. Such feelings—those of sadistic manipulation—were rare to him, but they were increasing. Briefly, an image of a fistfight between Buddy and Tony men flashed in his mind and it brought a smile to his face. It made him feel good, and he chuckled.

"Now wouldn't that be sumthin'. Tony would put him in his place and send him back to Maryland or Delaware or wherever he said he's from," Grady thought.

The walk to work during the middle of the day was much different than the one in the morning. There seemed to be double the amount of people, and there was a general discourteousness about the whole scene. San Francisco, the living postcard that it was, filled and swelled with all kinds of people, from all over the world.

Today, Grady heard all kinds of accents and saw all kinds of faces as he walked into and through the heart of the tourists' euphoria. As a global tourist location, the city was perennially in the top 10. To keep pace with the mid-day crowds in and around Union Square, Grady felt the need to quicken his pace.

The tourists were often paying more attention to the landscapes and their cameras than to the pedestrian matters of their fellow men. The number of black people Grady saw was even a little greater now, because of the sheer volume of people in the streets. But, as usual, they were dwarfed by the mostly white and Asian hordes. Grady continued to quicken his steps and he found himself glad that he worked the morning shift most of the time.

Work today turned out to be a refuge of calm. He and Marko worked well together. Closer in age, each man knew and conducted his responsibilities well. Differences in race and nationalities notwithstanding, the fact that the two men had lived longer lives than many around them seemed to give them a bond.

Despite what transpired between Grady and the old woman a day before, older people, like Grady and Marko, could sometimes relate on a certain level where life experiences transcended differences and borders. Regardless of all other factors, an old man is an old man and an old woman is an old woman with little strife left to live for, but with only memories left for reflection or regret. Sometimes these feelings and ideas were mutual and relatable between those approaching retirement. Despite age, perhaps it was also that Grady felt more comfortable around Marko *because* he was Russian, and not American.

In any case, these two got along well, displaying more teamwork than ever displayed between Grady and Buddy. Grady also worked well with Tony on those days when Tony filled in, but with Grady and Marko, there was more essential and genuine camaraderie. When Marko would take a break, for example, Grady would not leave his post until Marko returned; when Grady patrolled the building floors, Marko would be there to handle visitors and tenants in a matured, professional, and respectful manner. In all, the afternoon and evening went smoothly, and Grady felt very relaxed.

At 7 pm, Grady performed his regular duties, checking the video monitors, greeting visitors, bidding tenants farewell for the day, and filling out paperwork, as the lobby traffic dwindled. Around this time, the lobby doors were locked, and people could only enter by appointment or with a building security card. As Grady finished locking the doors, Marko took his turn to patrol the floors. Grady was working with Marko in the first place because Marko's usual partner needed the night off.

As part of working the afternoon shift, one guard was free to leave at 9pm, when the lobby traffic slowed overall. The other would stay until 11 pm to hand off responsibilities to the graveyard shift guard. Grady knew that Marko had a wife to get home to and he would let him be the one to go at 9 pm. Tomorrow Grady would be off anyway, to return on Thursday morning for his regular day shift, where he would be working with Tony.

Eventually, Marko changed from his uniform and was ready to leave for the evening. As he shuffled toward the exit he said, "Brought my umbrella, my wife thought it would rain. Sometimes she's right, sometimes she's wrong," and his face broke into a frumpy smile.

Grady smiled too. "Better to be on the safe side. Have a good night my friend," he said.

Marko waved one last time and left for the day. Typically, Marco would linger for 15-20 minutes to chat with Big Eric and members of his cleaning staff, who virtually took over the building after 8 pm. They were all Mexican and most of them spoke no English, but Marko had learned how to communicate with them over time. However, Marko left on time today, leaving Grady behind the desk with the computer screens and video monitors for the last two hours.

During that time housekeepers with buffers and vacuum cleaners, the building engineer, the elevator repairman, and late-working tenants came and went through the lobby. Despite those comings and goings, and the general activity around him, Grady could relax a little before his walk home. He read the newspaper and filled out his shift reports.

About 11:30 pm, after completing his final paperwork, Grady found himself again out on the streets of San Francisco, ready for the walk home. It was cool and windy, with light moisture in the air. It was not thick like fog, but it cast pallor over anything more than about 30 feet away. It was the kind of night air that Grady liked, a kind that contributed to the city's mythical reputations of mystery and romance. It was the kind of night that had charmed Grady and his wife into remaining in the city years ago, after they had been there for only a short while.

After working the swing shift, Grady would usually exit the building through its loading dock, instead of going through the front and the hassle of all its security. The loading dock exit put him right near where Sansome, Market, and Sutter Streets converged. The streets at this time of night, a time when Grady rarely found himself outdoors, were typically empty.

San Francisco entertained many activities during the daylight hours but it was not New York City. In general, San Francisco tended to turn in early. The exotic city with its fancy reputation for excess and waywardness was really a small town where people actually exercised their unique forms of depravity during decent hours.

It was a curious city of contrasts, blending often conservative social traditions and manners with equally powerful traditions of decadence and corruption. The city at the time had one of the highest automobile hit and run averages per capita in the country, where drivers, in their modern day haste to get to things trivial, would take the life of some pedestrian downtown, never stopping to take inventory of the carnage.

But now, almost nearing midnight, the city was relatively quiet, with an odd bus churning through the streets, a homeless person staggering by, urinating or picking through garbage, or a solo employee, like Grady, trying to get home.

After making sure the loading dock door closed behind him, Grady bundled up and tried to focus on getting home. Sutter Street was a straight shot to his apartment.

However, as he turned to head north, he could not help but notice someone walking on the other side of the street rather briskly. Though he could not see the face, the well-dressed man looked Asian, from the jet-black color and texture of his hair and the way that he walked. After living in San Francisco for a number of years, one could even learn to determine ethnicity from a distance.

To Grady, the man almost seemed to be walking too fast though and his shoes, which complimented a swaying and graceful overcoat, made clip clop sounds from their pounding of the sidewalk. They were loud enough to echo off the buildings and resonate in Grady's ears solidly with each step, even from all the way across the street. As Grady paralleled the man's steps, he was unable to stop himself from noting a stereotype he had developed over the years: "Chinese people don't usually walk that fast. I wonder why that boy's in such a big hurry."

Grady kept walking on his own side of the street toward home, gradually putting some distance between himself and the man. But then, suddenly, he had to stop, and turn sharply in the man's direction, drawn there by what sounded like a sharp and abrupt exchange of voices. From his vantage point, now about three quarters the way up the block, Grady could see that there were now two men. One of them still appeared to be the fast-walking Asian man, who now appeared to be in a loud and heated discussion with another man.

The San Francisco air and light winds muffled the men's voices somewhat, seeming to send what they said in different directions. However, Grady could still hear some words, and they did not sound pleasant.

Sensing a potential conflict, Grady crept back down the block close to the sides of the buildings on his side of the street, a little closer to the scene of what was happening. There appeared to be no one else around, only streetlights, tall buildings, and a few brake lights in the distance.

The Asian man had been walking fast, but Grady had not considered that he was headed toward some kind of altercation. Meanwhile, as Grady watched while he walked, the Asian man seemed to try to step around the other man, to continue on his way. The second man, however, appeared to deliberately insinuate himself into the Asian man's path.

This is not the San Francisco way, Grady thought. The city was too sedate when it came to conflict; even high-volume arguments were generally rare. No, Grady pondered as he got a little closer, this was something different.

When he got to within a quarter of a block, he could see that the other man was a white man, also in a long overcoat, and with a briefcase on the ground next to him. Suddenly, as Grady watched, the two men became locked into a heated, face-to-face exchange, not unlike a baseball manager and umpire. Grady could tell now that the Asian man was shorter, by what seemed like five inches.

"I'm not listening anymore, mate. These ah gonna to do my talking soon," the white man said, referring to his fists, which he raised while Grady watched. His comment made Grady chuckle. "I'm going to pummel you if you don't address your attitude," the angry white man added.

"You bumped into me. Look at my shoe. You owe me an apology," the smaller Asian man responded.

Grady was hiding in a doorway across the street, from where he could now see and hear the sounds of the confrontation precisely. He could tell that the white man had a foreign accent, but he was not exactly sure from where. Then he suddenly saw the Asian man physically push the strange-talking white man, in response to the man's threat.

"I warned you, mate," the white man said quickly before aggressively grabbing the Asian man around the neck and putting him into a headlock. Up to this point, it all had been somewhat comical for Grady, but he was totally unprepared for what happened next. Rather barbarically and savagely and without warning, the white man took the Asian man's head, still in the headlock position, and rammed it hard into the side of the building they were near.

The action resembled a move from a television wrestling match, and it was swift and brutal. The Asian man and his head were used like a battering ram. It was a hasty and violent culmination to whatever had precipitated the altercation.

Grady continued to watch, in shock but still for the theater of it all, with downtown San Francisco as the stage. The Asian man, after being rammed into the wall, immediately slumped to the sidewalk in a heap next to the building.

The white man stood over his victim for several moments. Then Grady saw the white man, after kicking at his opponent's body with his foot several times for signs of life, pick up his briefcase and begin a rather calm walk over to Grady's side of the street.

Instinctively, Grady buried himself deeper into the shadow of the doorway. He was not afraid. He was not really sure how he felt. But with his continued anonymity, he felt a sense of potential significance coming on and he wanted to preserve it.

So he let the white man pass, and was able to get a good look at him.

The white man was tall. His coat was dark blue, black, or brown. He had reddish-brown hair and thick, prominent eyebrows that were a shade darker. His mustache matched the unusual color of his eyebrows. He was about Grady's height, perhaps a little taller.

As he passed under a streetlamp, his face blazed under the light. However, his face still appeared relatively calm, despite what he had done. Quickly, Grady thought that he could pick this man out a lineup if need be. But for now, he let him march up the street to whatever world he was going to inhabit. What else could he do at the moment? The crime was now over, as it had happened so quickly. The rest would be up to the police. Grady could have come out of the shadows and confronted the man before he walked away, but to what end? The man was younger and obviously angry. Grady might not stand a chance under such conditions. He could pass on information to the police later.

As soon as the man was gone from sight and the wind had absorbed the clip clop of his shoes, Grady edged his head out into the light and viewed the body across the street. It was not moving. Then, almost unconsciously, Grady looked down at his uniform, at what he himself was wearing. Though he did not know what *irony* was exactly, the fact that he was a security guard made him feel inadequate, yet responsible and qualified at the same time. He did not carry a weapon or have a badge, but he was in the security business nevertheless. Yet all of his authority was restricted to one building, was it not?

All of his power was limited to polite, but strongly emphasized requests from building tenants and visitors. He had no responsibility to average citizens. They were on their own. Still, the fact that he was wearing the uniform at all compelled him to do something, something important or official, and so he walked slowly across the street to see the body. Strangely, there was still no one else in sight on the streets. It was just he, the body, the tall buildings, and the San Francisco air, which seemed to have its own movement and presence, as usual. The city was watching him if no one or nothing else was, to see what he would do next, to gauge his moral courage in a place where no such courage was necessarily required.

Grady decided that if he were going to call the police, perhaps he should at least examine the man's body first. Perhaps there was some aid the man might need before Grady moved off to find a pay phone or went back to his building to use one there. CPR training had been a part of his guard orientation, though it had been at least a year since that training. As he approached, meanwhile, he noticed that the man continued to lay still.

Suddenly, a powerful wind gust moving down Sutter Street to Market Street seemed to push him down toward the intersection with Sansome Street and away from the body. But he gathered himself to the point where he was eventually standing over the man.

The man was Asian all right. He was probably Chinese and was very well dressed, from his shoes on up to his head. He appeared to be unconscious, but Grady hesitated to bend down and examine the man, so he stayed upright. From that vantage point and with the man's head mostly in a shadow, Grady could not see a wound or blood, and that was fine with him. Grady thought out loud, "Whatever happened must a' happened inside his head. Hey man you all right!" he said, poking the Asian man with his toe, looking for a reaction. There was none.

He quickly looked back up the block to see if the other man might be returning to the scene out of remorse or to cover his tracks in some way. "Thas cole blooded," Grady mumbled to himself, after seeing no one, only several cars moving through the intersection along the above street. "People today are jus' cole blooded."

He struggled with the idea that he should check the man for breathing and signs of life, but this meant touching him, and Grady was not sure he wanted to do that. Perhaps he should find a cop or call an ambulance; time was probably critical at this point.

The man looked so polished and well-groomed, resembling the kind of people that traversed the lobby in Grady's building from day-to-day. Some of those people were arrogant snobs, who would not even give Grady the time of day, just taking him for granted and assuming his automatic cooperation, respect, loyalty, and service -- like the guy who had asked him to get the card table yesterday.

Yes, it was true: some of them were nice, but most were not. Some were even outright disrespectful and mean at times. What about the woman who had called him a "nigger" just yesterday also, Alzheimer's disease or not? "Too much money can make you mean and nasty," he mumbled to himself, looking again at the crisply starched pink collar of the man's shirt, his rich brown, leather shoes, one of which appeared scuffed, and the dull glow they still reflected off the hovering street light. The man's watch was a silver, chain-linked piece with a rich reflective blue surface for showing the time.

Plus, he was Asian. This was the first Asian person Grady had ever studied up close. He had lived among the Asians for decades now and he generally got along with them, but he had still only really known them from a distance. They were people in his building, in the supermarkets, and on the buses, but he had not interacted with them in a real, intimate way. He could not really say that he had any special loyalty to Asian people. He felt no connection between his old black self and this young man's Asian self.

Besides, what had happened was between *them*—a white person and an Asian one—and not him. It had been a battle of wealth: the rich, well-dressed Asian man and the rich, well-dressed White man, where, this round at least, the Asian man had lost. Their two races ran the world anyway. What business of theirs was his? Let them fight their own battles between them. They lived in and had created their world and now they had to operate by its rules, tragic though it might have become.

Standing there being buffeted by sudden, powerful wind gusts, he decided that the man was too much of a lot of things that Grady was not, to be touched. "No. I don't want nothin' to do with this," he said, alternating looks between the body and up the street where the other man had disappeared. Something in him, or perhaps around him, supplanted his waning compassion with apathy and disdain, sealing that compassion off perhaps for the immediate future.

"This don't have nothin' to do with me," he reinforced to himself. "This ain't none of my business when you really get down to it. They rich. I ain't. They can handle their own business. They good at that," he mumbled and then he backed away as if he was now fleeing a crime scene of his own making. He kept moving backward until he was across the street staring at the Asian man's body from a distance, and then he began a slow trek home.

CHAPTER V

Grady could not get it all out of his mind as he walked home. He was, after all, human. There was a wounded, maybe even a dead man lying in street, just a block from where he worked, and Grady had witnessed the incident that resulted in the man's injuries. What could he do now, now that he had decided to do nothing?

It might be said that his decision had been colored by his developing anger and apathy over life. As far as he was concerned, he was simply fed up with the world and its ways lately. It was not worth saving. It seemed to be more worth destroying, if anything. As for compassion and civic responsibility, those feelings had been on their way out anyway.

Grady considered that it was *their* world that had probably created the conditions that led to the altercation and *their* world which led to his decision and current ways of thinking. It was a rough world and he was only playing by *their* rules. They were the ones who made the rules. They operated in theirs and he would operate in his. He might work in and for their world, but that was the extent of his obligation.

Then there was the case of the black boy being shot in the back by the police over in Oakland. That did not help matters in his mind. Let the upper classes handle their own affairs. He wanted it left at that. But what would he do? He would wait, he thought to himself, as cold winds buffeted him while he walked.

Shortly after crossing Montgomery Street, he started to see faces, mostly white faces. He thought that maybe one of them might trickle down to Sansome Street and discover the body. That would perhaps be *apropos*. He wondered if the attacker himself was somewhere nearby, looking out a window while sipping on a drink, thinking about what he did, maybe even planning a return to the scene after his drink to watch the police in morbid fascination.

A drink, as a matter of fact, seemed like a good idea on this chilly night, so Grady stopped by one of the stores near his home, which he frequented. As he entered the store, a new sensation came over him that he had never had before, or had not had in a while. All of a sudden, he felt powerful. Did he not, all of a sudden, hold the keys to life and death, in a certain way? He had seen something that no one else had seen and he knew the truth, or at least he knew *a* truth, something that no one else knew.

Pridefully, after taking his time in the aisles to find something, he walked up to the counter and placed down a bottle of white wine, instead of his usual cheap liquor and beer, feeling that he preferred wine tonight. With the day off tomorrow, he would settle down and relax tonight, maybe cook a little something to eat with the window open, because he wanted to let San Francisco inside his world tonight. It was welcome tonight, for he was now a member of a new class. He had tasted the power that others seemed to perpetually enjoy, and he would raise his glass in a toast with his genuine friend, the city itself.

He already knew the Arab man behind the store counter, but this night Grady was even more familiar, gregarious, and talkative, than usual. His conscience regarding what he had witnessed still existed, but it was now being suppressed by strange new feelings of being "special." Part of him wanted to tell the store owner what he had seen, but the other part was not ready to do that yet, if ever. So, he broached the subject, ever so cautiously.

"Crime really gettin' bad in this city. Can't even walk the streets," he said, offhandedly, clumsily trying to stir up conversation.

"Very bad," the balding, middle-aged man concurred. "Yes, very, very bad. Not enough jobs for everybody." He took a quick look at the bottle, knowing some of Grady's drinking habits by heart. "You drinking the good stuff now ay?" he said, adding a short laugh and grin.

Grady shared in the laugh. "Why not? I'm off tomorrow. Thought I would take it easy and relax tonight. People like us deserve a break too."

The man was not exactly sure what Grady was referencing, but kept the brief conversation going nonetheless.

"No problem there my friend" the store owner said. "You have big plans tomorrow? Or are you going to sleep? Sleep is always good."

"Not sure right now," Grady said, feeling, in a slightly paranoid way, that the man was suddenly prying into his business. "Gonna take it one step at a time my man. No rush."

The man smiled and bagged Grady's purchase.

Grady wasn't sure exactly what he was going to do when he woke up in the morning and the comment got him thinking about the next day in general. "Let me get this too," he said, picking up a copy of the San Francisco Chronicle and slipping 50 cents into the man's hand on the way out of the store. When Grady left, the man turned his back to business as usual.

On the sidewalk, as he continued to walk under a foggy, late, light, and early spring mist, Grady listened for sirens. A strong pang of guilt grabbed him upon this awareness. With his left hand, he grasped for his chest, over where his heart would be, and he felt tightness underneath, along with a numbness spreading down his right arm.

He continued to walk, pushing for home, as the tightness proved to be a short-lived spasm. He felt bad for the Asian man, but the man was on his own, like all creatures were ultimately.

Nevertheless, thoughts continued to wade through his mind about the crime. If the man's body was to be discovered around this time, sirens would be the strongest indication and their sounds might be heard even from his apartment, some eight blocks away. Downtown San Francisco was hollow and had acoustics like that. A single sound could go a long way. But he heard nothing so far.

Perhaps by now, some homeless person was rifling through the man's pockets, taking his wallet, shoes, watch and especially his coat for warmth, maybe even stripping him clean. Meanwhile, people were leaving bars in the neighborhood, many consciously oblivious to the homeless and junkies lying in the streets beneath them.

Amid these observations, Grady briefly had an image of the Asian man on the sidewalk naked, stripped bare by the desperate, scavenging world in which he lived. The man then would not only have lost his life by means of murder, but he might be profaned in the streets as well, completely defiled and humiliated after being attacked.

Surely there would be a siren soon, Grady thought as he continued to walk away toward the safety of home, wine bottle and newspaper held tightly in his hand, against his body.

A strange instinct had made him purchase the newspaper. He thought he might find some news of the man's demise as soon as he got home, but that was impossible as the paper had been published before the incident. Thinking of this, he tossed the paper into a garbage can about a block away from his apartment. "I don't need this," he thought to himself. "I'll buy one tomorrow to see if anything is in it."

When Grady got to his building, he saw that the building manager was in his office, behind the Plexiglas window, near the entrance. He was not usually there during the week, and this would be a good time to ask the big white man about the dimming hallway light bulb, which might have gone out by now. But Grady, for some reason he could not explain, wanted to be more talkative than that. He felt the need to relate to another human being, in a more substantive way. Forgetting about the bulb, he decided to learn about McTeague, with whom he had had limited conversations to this point. To go along with his large frame and white hair, McTeague had tattoos of snakes, roses, and anchors on his massive pink-white arms.

"Where you from McTeague?" Grady asked after finding out that the manager was there just to address some minor building concerns.

"Born in Placer County, but lived most of my life here in San Francisco," he said, and he had a twang in his voice that was not quite southern, but something completely born out of the West. "Spent some years down in the southland -- LA and San Diego -- but ended up back here."

"Couldn't get away from the City by the Bay, could ya?" Grady asked, completely unaware that he had expressed his words in a singsong, rhyming fashion.

"San Francisco is a stage where you can be any character you want to be," McTeague said, getting suddenly philosophical at almost 12:30 pm on a Tuesday. "Here people perform for each other. Sometimes people look to see what you are doing and you do the same for them so that everyone feels that they are welcome and appreciated. Everybody is happy because everybody wants everybody else to be happy. In some ways, San Francisco is an altar where people worship together."

"And also" he added, "no matter what you did in your past, San Francisco never remembers. It always gives you a clean slate. It never judges you. But some people say San Francisco is evil. Yea, maybe so. But so is the rest of the world. We're just more honest about it, and that's the way I feel about that?"

Grady responded in the only way he felt reasonable at the moment: "Didn't know you were such a heavy thinker, McTeague. I've never heard you talk much." He was surprised at the cascade of information coming from the building manager, who also had pale, colorless eyes, which made him look ghostly.

"Learned a lot over the years," McTeague said. "A whole lot. More than ya know."

At that precise moment, as if McTeague's comment had set off a kind of tripwire, the sound of sirens blared somewhere in the distance, loud enough for both men to hear. Grady felt that it was time for him to get up to his room. It was getting late anyway, now approaching 1 a.m.

"Well I'm glad to hear that," the black man said. "Might as well get the most out of life before it's all over." Grady never mentioned the lightbulb before going up to his room, though he felt satisfied after having had two conversations with other human beings. He had needed them.

When Grady got to his hallway under the still-dimming bulb's flickering light, he managed to see the white edge of an envelope under his door. Inside the envelope was a letter from his daughter; it was something about her needing him to contact her about her housing issues.

After reading further, he learned that she specifically needed him to come over to the complex where she lived to sign some paperwork so that she and his grandson could continue to receive federal housing aid and remain where they were living. This thing happened every few years and Grady had done the same thing the last time

His daughter, Ruth, said in the letter, "As soon as possible, maybe Saturday," as she knew that he was off on the weekends. This would mean he would have to take a bus to see her Saturday morning and aid her situation. In any case, she had told him to call her and there was a number at the bottom of the note. To read the note completely, he had to step into his apartment for additional light as the hallway bulb continued to flicker desperately. In the back of his mind, he resolved to make the sacrifice and get a new bulb tomorrow, instead of going back downstairs to ask McTeague tonight. He was inside now and did not feel like going back out into the world.

Once completely inside his apartment, more sirens from outside his window shook him back into consciousness. This time they were right outside his window, racing directly down Sutter Street. It could only be the crime he had witnessed, he thought, and he rushed over to the window to catch a glimpse of an ambulance racing beneath, assaulting his ears with its wails. To his surprise, following behind, there appeared a single police squad car, followed even more dramatically by what appeared to be a television news truck.

Quickly, Grady went to the TV set to turn on the news, only to realize that the late evening news had been off for over an hour. He would have to wait until morning. He thought about the newspaper and wondered what its headline might read in a few hours.

Before going to bed, he poured himself a large glass of wine, moved a chair in front of the open window, placed his feet up on the ledge, and symbolically toasted with the San Francisco air.

As he got drunk, he felt a more potent kind of intoxication. It was laced with the power he was feeling. Through his window, he reinforced his oneness with the darker element of the city, the black heart that seduced human nature with pride, unforgiveness, and revenge.

"It ain't my problem," he mumbled to himself. "Is theirs. Les' see how they handle it. Hopefully better than that boy over in Oakland."

CHAPTER VI

The wine and the city seemed to agree with one another about his new feelings of power and control; and though he did not get much sleep that night, he still felt rested when he awoke the following morning. At first, he did not even think about what happened the night before. The wine had something to do with that, but mostly he found himself caught up in that nebulous fog that a new day brings, where people have to get their bearings before they can begin to perceive reality, whether it be past, present, or future.

This activity, however, was interrupted by the reality around him, in the form of the banging and clanging of pots from across the hall, designed specifically to annoy neighbors. Lorraine was trying to stir up some early morning trouble again and this would soon be followed by the rumbling of feet from upstairs. All this made Grady angry this time because he wanted to watch the news in peace. He thought about going out into the hall to get Lorraine to stop, since she seemed to be the instigator this morning.

Outside the window, a drowsy, light rain fell, and the mist from it seemed to induce sleepiness from its very observation.

So, with the distracting and annoying morning sounds hitting him intermittently, and the soft rain coming down, he sat in front of the television hoping to see if anything was being reported about the injured Asian man he had left in the street. News of this might dictate how he might schedule his day.

He didn't see anything about an Asian man being found in the street last night; but it was now the middle of the newscast, so maybe it had already been reported and would be repeated later. That was the way the news usually worked he had learned over the years.

While he waited, he opened his window to the fire escape and breathed in the morning air. He needed it. Lorraine was still clanging across the hall. It was almost 8 am and the world, as usual, was preparing for its day, with the sounds of buses, cars, trash trucks, and human voices competing for attention. Combined with these sounds was the light pelting sounds of the rain from the white-gray sky.

He heard a spontaneous and unusual shout from someone below echo all the way up to the rooftop. But, as was often, he could not tell if it was an expression of thunderous joy, rage, or madness. The Hispanic family was getting into their morning routine and Grady started to hear the familiar rumbling sounds from upstairs. Grady closed the window to keep the rain out of his apartment. Meanwhile, Lorraine continued her sporadic kitchenware tirade. "Yep, I'm on their side this mornin'," Grady said to himself.

Obviously, there was a new verbal fight brewing between the neighbors, and Grady again decided to go to his door to see it. There was nothing else to do while he waited for the news. If nothing else, what he saw might provide an entertaining deviation from the serious concerns of last night.

As he looked into the hall, he suddenly saw the Hispanic father pass by his door; after which he distinctly heard the promise, "I will return *señora. Yo regreso.*" The man was alone and was heading off down the hall, to somewhere Grady could not figure, leaving Lorraine and her noise behind, with only another threat. He had not looked in the direction of Grady's cracked door.

"Where's he goin'"? Grady thought. "Maybe he's gonna get a gun or some of his friends to break down her door. She pro'bly deserves it at this point."

After that thought, looking through the crack in his door again, Grady noticed Lorraine open her door slowly and carefully. He had not spoken to her since the last morning altercation.

This morning, however, out of desire to find out what was going on, or the desire to just say "hello" to a neighbor, Grady decided to open his door and confront her about the noise and the Hispanic father. He wanted to at least see what she had to say for herself. His television continued to blare in the background, but he would get back to it shortly. The morning news would be on for the next few hours, and then there was a noon news hour, and a five o'clock, and a six o'clock news. The news was always on these days, compared to when he was younger. It was a busy and talkative world. He would discover the information he needed one way or the other.

Lorraine was wearing faded blue jeans and a white, cotton blouse with frilly cuffs. Her stringy hair was uncombed and looked like brown steel wool as it reached down past her shoulders. She wore no shoes. Overall, she did not look bad in Grady's mind; in fact, she looked like a person who could have been doing better, but had perhaps given up trying.

"What's goin' on this mawnin'?" Grady asked. He was less careful about his speech away from work, but Lorraine wasn't the type that would appreciate the effort anyway.

She had a self-satisfied look on her face. "You probably heard me plenty this morning. Well, all I can say is that the first time it happened, I was only looking for some pans so I could cook somethin'."

She was now out in the hall where Grady could clearly get a look at her. Her brown eyes were defiant, direct, and even challenging. She held a gaze that seemed to be possessed by even the most despondent of white people.

"But then, like usual, he and his family take it the wrong way," she continued, breathless. "Those people are too sensitive, don't you think? Who do they think they are anyway?"

"Leave me out of all that," Grady said, stopping her, "But you need to keep it down, baby. Other people live heah too," he added through a forced smile. "Like me. Also," he continued, "You better be careful. You don't know what people will do these days, what they capable of now. 'Specially in this neighborhood."

But then he caught himself, because he had just seen a brutal attack in the wealthy Financial District where he worked, proving that violence could defy class; and as this thinking made clear the democracy and reality of everyday violence in his mind, it also reminded him that it was time to get back to the TV set to see the news.

"Where you think he went?" Grady posed before leaving her in the hall.

"Couldn't care less," Lorraine responded dismissively. "He can go wherever he wants. Him and his family."

"I don't want to see nothin' happen to you," Grady said, now almost at his apartment door. "We been living here a while now and I'm used to you." He chuckled a bit, and his smile was genuine this time.

"Ain't nothing gonna happen to me," she said. "I'm still white, ain't I? That still counts for something in this world." After she said this, she herself laughed at what she thought was clever.

Grady was not surprised by what she said. He expected it from her. She could be blunt about race in general, and part of him respected that.

"Yea, you're white, but that don't mean as much as it used to mean. Everybody wants a piece nowadays, and they means to get it."

"I got no problem sharing with people. This is a big enough country for everybody. Just don't try to tell me what to do and how to live, and show me the respect I deserve."

Grady did not feel like arguing with her any further. It was like talking to a child in some ways. "I'll keep an ear at the door and an eye at the peephole," he said.

"Come out if you hear me screaming," Lorraine said sardonically and then laughed out loud. She added, "Don't worry Jonas. The world is still on my side," and she laughed again.

For Grady this time though, such a comment left the realm of the humorous and started to smack of superiority and arrogance, making him think of his early days in the South and of the incident that had taken place two days ago with the old woman in his building lobby. White people still had a long way to go, he thought. They still thought they were invincible. Perhaps they would never learn. Or maybe they would need to learn the hard way.

Hoping there would be no more problems this morning, Grady threw a wave up in the air to acknowledge he had heard her before entering his apartment. It was now time to find out what had happened last night. He did not have to wait long. At precisely 8:30 am, one of the local news broadcasts led off with the story of a man whose body had been found late last night at the corner of Sutter and Sansome Streets.

CHAPTER VII

The man, whose name had been Edward Chen, was, in fact, dead, perhaps losing his life sometime between 11 and 1 am, the news people said. His body had been found exactly where Grady had left him. Grady observed the picture they had up on the screen. The face he had seen last night had been cocked to the side against the sidewalk and deep in shadow, preventing a really good look.

Chen, 31, was a handsome young fellow who had a wife and two children. Grady was amazed at the speed with which the news media had gathered a small fortune of information on the man's life and background. It had only been a few hours. As he watched the images of police, fire officials, reporters, and street scenes recorded from last night, the talking female reporter recounted the information on Chen through narration.

Chen, who was, in fact, Chinese, had been vice president of his family's real estate firm, which was located in an office building on Sansome Street, just two blocks from where his body was found, and only a few blocks away from where Grady worked. The police said that Chen had been at a bar on Montgomery Street earlier in the evening and had gone back to his office to retrieve some paperwork that he had meant to take to his home in the San Francisco avenues. This information had been provided by his wife, Jennifer, who appeared saddened on the screen while being interviewed by a news reporter.

She had been waiting for her husband at the bar. His body had been found by one of the MUNI bus drivers whose route turned the corner from Sansome to Sutter. Grady could not estimate how soon after he had left that the body had been found and did not even try, as a twinge of guilt shot through him while listening to the report. But his guilt passed by like a wave that buffets and then recedes from a shore, as it was quickly replaced by a fascination with what he was watching unfold, something of which he was uniquely a part. So, he continued to listen and watch, mildly entranced.

To Grady, Chen looked not unlike many other Chinese men in San Francisco. In the absence of ever getting to know one on a personal level, he tended to view them in a general and collective way, in terms of looks, attitudes, and behaviors. This man appeared to be yet another Asian with whom Grady might have had little contact with in life.

He had not expected the barrage of information he was getting to come so quickly, as if he was now being forced to make a decision, to come forward with what he knew. It was like he was rapidly becoming the missing piece of some puzzle. He still tried to remain calm to learn more about what had happened. However, his concentration was broken when he heard another commotion outside his door.

"Police, open your door please!"

He jumped up and stood in place first. Then he walked slowly towards the door. When got there, he looked through the peephole.

There was no one there. Then, he heard voices in the hallway.

Cracking his door again, he saw two uniformed officers outside Lorraine's door. She had not yet opened it. The hallway light was still dim because of the flickering bulb, but behind the two police was the Hispanic father.

"He got the police," Grady surmised in mild disbelief. "And they came." But he didn't want to leave the television set and miss any more of the news broadcast.

However, before he could leave his door, he heard "What is it!" uttered brashly from the direction of where the three men stood. It was a female voice, so it had to be Lorraine. "I didn't do nothin'."

"We're here to look into a complaint. Please open your door, ma'am."

Lorraine opened her door, but Grady could not wait to hear what would transpire. He had to get back to the television because he wanted to hear more about the police investigation. So, he hustled back over to his chair instead. Continuing to watch the broadcast, he learned that there were no suspects and no apparent witnesses to what had happened last night.

The news reporter pointed her microphone at Edward Chen's wife for a last-minute plea for information on her husband's apparent murder. The reporter explained further that the police also had no apparent motive for what had happened.

Additionally Chen, despite all that he had been wearing, had not been robbed. He had been found fully clothed, with his wallet and other personal and expensive belongings intact. Perhaps, like Grady, someone else might have been intimidated by Chen's apparent wealth and did not want to approach him.

The police, meanwhile, would only grudgingly speculate that a murder had, in fact, occurred. It was the media that was central in promoting this possibility. The precise manner of death had not even been officially determined, though Grady did hear the words, "possibly due to severe head trauma."

Taking it all in, Grady was still amazed at how quickly information and the histories of certain people's lives could be accumulated and processed for public consumption. He wondered how much information could be gathered about his own life had he been the victim, or if anyone would have even bothered.

Then Grady stopped to recall, as images of the previous night migrated back into his brain. The blow administered by the harsh-looking white man with dark and reddish burnt eyebrows, and a matching mustache, had been quick and powerful. That man, Grady remembered, had been tall, seeming to use all his height as leverage to crash the shorter Chen's head into the building's wall. The attack was quick, merciless, and cruel. The man then had just calmly walked away. Didn't he deserve to be brought to justice and punished?

As the remaining information spilled from the TV screen, the fact that he might be the key to the whole investigation began to dawn on Grady. He needed more time to think about what to do. If the victim had been black, he might have reported it right away. Maybe. But whites and Asians had it all in San Francisco. What did he owe to them, despite the tears that had flowed from the eyes of Edward Chen's wife? But who had soothed the tears of many black wives back in his day when their husbands were found swinging from trees? Where was the justice then? What about Arthur Grant over in Oakland? What kind of justice was he getting now? Whites were racist then; they were racist now too weren't they, just in a different way. The Asians were in on it as well. No, he would not report what he had seen, he suddenly and defiantly determined in his soul, as he continued to sit in front of the TV screen.

As the news story fed into a commercial, he stretched and began to think about what he was going to do next. Then he remembered the police in the hallway, and he thought about going back to his door to see what was taking place. But instead of following through with either thought, he opened his window and stepped out onto his fire escape. He needed fresh air again.

Immediately, he was greeted by cooing pigeons perched on the edge of the roof of the opposing building. They were fluttering and seeming to look down on him.

He did not like pigeons in general. They were too pervasive and intrusive. But he ignored them for the moment because taking in the air was essential at this point and it felt good this morning, as it did most mornings. Rarely was the San Francisco air one's enemy. It was what you did with it that mattered.

Meanwhile, he still had not decided how he would spend the day off from work. He decided he would think about that as he got dressed and he went inside to see what was going on out in the hall. Taking a glance at the television again as he worked his way to his door, he saw that the news story had ended.

When he got back to the door, he heard muffled voices outside. He cracked the door open to check on the goings on and he saw all the interested parties at play. The two policemen stood between Lorraine, who was inside her doorway, and the Hispanic father, who still stood behind the officers. The father stood erect and silent, but Lorraine's arms were gesticulating. Grady could not make out her words, so he knew that the police had convinced her to talk in her normal voice, instead of shouting.

As he watched the tiresome neighbor conflict again, a thought crossed his mind: *Maybe I can tell 'em about last night. I can get it over with and get on with my life. I could say I was scared. No, but then they might think I was crazy and had something to do with it. I can't trust the police.*

The awkwardness over such a late admission and his growing belief that he was actually making a statement in favor of the underclass in *not* reporting what he had seen, overwhelmed this brief impulse to provide information on what he knew.

If he felt a twinge of guilt over not reporting the crime, it did not take up more space in his subconscious than the sense of revenge against an elitist society, which he also possessed. That inclination was still being buoyed by the growing sense of vanity in his new position, as a key witness to a crime. With all this in mind, he wanted to see how everything would play out in the end. *He* had not killed Chen. He had only *seen* who had done it. It was not his responsibility to catch a killer.

When the police left, he had time to think about what to do next. Part of him wanted to go over to see Lorraine to see what had happened, as he had been a part of that situation too, only a half hour ago. As a neighbor, he felt that he was in some way entitled to an explanation, but he opted against this. He did not feel like dealing with her again right now. She might end up wanting to talk about it too much and he had too much on his mind at the moment. Later he might ask her what had happened in passing.

He needed to get out, to walk, and to think. Perhaps then he might decide what to do about the larger dilemma he faced.

In the meantime, he would monitor how the investigation into Edward Chen's death progressed.

But at only 9 am Wednesday morning, it was a still a little too early to go out into the world, as far as he was concerned. People out in the world at this time were there for specific purposes, like work and tourism. He would feel like an outcast just sort of wandering around with no apparent aim.

He would wait until about noon when he would go down to the McDonald's on Market Street and see if his buddies might be there, including Wizard. Wizard was a supposed former college professor, whose knowledge Grady respected, even if Wizard could sometimes act a little erratic.

So, for the next several hours Grady slept, as best he could. In an uncharacteristic daytime move for him, he left the window open. He felt a desire again to bathe in the San Francisco air.

Once before when he did this, several pigeons flew inside and it took him a half hour to steer them back outside into the alley. Since he was on a fire escape, he also usually slept with the window closed because of his wariness of inviting intruders. But this morning, like last night, he felt that *he* had the power. The San Francisco air was in cooperation with this new self-image, and feeling the air gave him greater confidence. More than ever before, he felt he had established a new kind of bond or covenant with the city.

In a dream, he saw himself on the top of his office building, hundreds of feet in the air, almost in the clouds again. He was reading a newspaper while looking out over the city from time to time. The articles of the paper were there with the words, but the pictures were all blacked out, leaving only large blocks of ink where the pictures were supposed to be.

Standing there, the clouds vaporized, opening up to the sun and a bright, blue day. He continued to read the news stories, while occasionally looking down below at the ant-like population moving along their straight ant-trails, amongst the automobiles and mass transit.

When he awoke, driven out of his dream by a hot sun coming over the building roof, he had no idea what the dream meant, only that he felt powerful.

✑

He wanted to buy a newspaper on the way down to Market Street to get another perspective on the crime he had witnessed. He left for Market Street at 11:30. Out in the hallway, the dying bulb again flickered and he decided to definitely get a new one on the way back, if he could remember.

Down near the entrance, McTeague was dozing at his desk. He must have stayed all night, now dreaming his own dreams, of which Grady could not imagine. Looking at McTeague though Grady thought again of the killer, and Grady wondered where that man had gone. What did he do right after his crime? Had he seen the news, and if so, where was the man's mind now? Maybe Chen would be alive if the man had checked on him immediately, instead of casually walking away.

Grady turned himself onto the sidewalk and merged into the sea of people. A new thought intruded into his brain; was not Grady as guilty as the killer for not reporting the crime? Was there a law against *not* reporting a crime? He had not thought about this yet, but it seemed like a logical question. There were laws for everything. Was there not a crime related to his situation also?

He was not sure, but thought the whole idea silly and ignored it. Instead, his thoughts turned again to the killer. Was the man still in the city and if so, might he himself, like his victim, work somewhere nearby? Grady had not thought about this until now. Maybe the man worked downtown close to where Grady worked. He seemed dressed well enough and familiar enough with the downtown terrain. What if the man was, in fact, a neighborhood regular in San Francisco's downtown and what if he simply went to work the next day? It might be possible for Grady to cross paths with him again in the course of daily goings on, and what would he do if he saw the man again? He would cross that bridge when he came to it.

What was that word he had called Chen? It had not been "man," but "mate." Grady had heard the word before, but could not remember where. People from somewhere talk like that, he thought, but he could not remember where. In any case, he knew that he could identify the man if he saw him again. Apparently, Grady himself had not been seen by anyone. All these things popped into his head as he walked down Sutter to a newsstand to buy a paper.

Grady purchased a San Francisco Chronicle, and on the right side of the lower front page, Grady saw Edward Chen's face under the headline: **Businessman Found Dead Near Financial District Intersection.** Chen, smiling in the picture, looked healthy, happy, and polished.

Grady read the story as he walked, trying to avoid bumping into anyone as he did so:

> *A San Francisco real estate executive was found dead on a downtown street corner late last night, near an intersection in the heart of the city's financial district.*

Police, who found the body after being led there by a passing MUNI driver, said the man appeared to have died from a head injury, though they would not speculate on the exact cause of his death or the circumstances that might have led to it.

"We don't know right now," an unidentified officer at the scene said. "From the nature of the injury, and from what we have been able to determine so far, it does not appear that he slipped and hit his head. We also do not think that he jumped from the building's rooftop. We are looking at something else and that does not exclude possible foul play of some kind."

Police would not identify the man, but family members, among them the man's wife, identified him as Edward Chen, a San Francisco native, who lived with his family in the Richmond District. He was the vice president of his family's real estate firm, Chen and Chen Properties. The firm is among the city's most prestigious.

Jennifer Chen said she lived with her husband with their two children, next door to the home of Chen's parents. Chen's sister and her husband live in a house across the street.

"It is a family business and we are very close," his wife said, adding that Chen was a fifth generation San Franciscan who could trace his heritage all the way back to the 1860s when his ancestors first arrived from China and worked on the railroads.

Police added that they have no suspects and would not speculate on a series of events or a motive.

That was it. The whole story was contained on the front page in a little square box with the picture. Grady, after reading the brief article and now well into his head-clearing walk, tucked the paper under his arm and picked up his speed amongst the increasing crowd.

It was about half past noon now. As he reached Union Square, there were all kinds of people around him. He thought that maybe he should not have taken this particular route. This was the glamorous route, but there were other ways to get to Market Street that had less people. Though he did not feel like dealing with this many people this was, in fact, the shortest route to his destination. He continued to wade through the masses.

Among the people he saw, there was no shortage of Asians. Grady had never really learned to tell the difference between Chinese, Japanese, Vietnamese, Filipino, or Korean by sight. He did not know if he would ever master such visual acuity. However, upon seeing the different Asian faces hurriedly file by, he spent a little more time staring at those faces, wondering if there were physical differences, or if they were all just Asian. He subconsciously tucked the paper more tightly under his arm.

Asians had never done anything to him, he could not help but ponder as he walked. They had always been fair with him. There were many he had met and liked over the years, since moving to California. They were disciplined, hard-working, and even-tempered. It was the whites and his own people who had presented whatever difficulties he had with people in his life, between growing up in the South and during his life out West.

White people, from time to time, had tried to *keep* him down; and black people on several occasions over the years, had tried to *bring* him down. So what was his problem with Asians? There was none, he considered. It was the big picture of society he was looking at, the corporate part, the monied part, the privileged part.

The Asians, especially in San Francisco, were a part of all those things. It was not a racial thing, or even a personal thing, but a sociological thing, though he was not able put such concepts into words of his own. It was just something he felt.

It was indeed getting back at the proverbial "man." At the very least it was allowing "the man" to take care of business in his own world, while Grady and the people in his lower-class world handled business in their own. It was a class thing, not a race thing, though the two were always confused and often related.

Grady thought of his daughter as he continued his walk to Market Street. Her life perhaps epitomized the lower-class struggle with life. The stark contrast of her existence in comparison to Edward Chen's wife, Jennifer, could not be more vivid, and here was Grady, the man that they both needed for help.

Again, these were all things that he *felt,* but was not able necessarily to articulate as philosophy. If Wizard was at the McDonald's, he would ask him about it. Grady looked forward with anticipation to that conversation.

CHAPTER VIII

It was another beautiful day. The kind of day where San Francisco seemed to twinkle like a jewel. He had come to love San Francisco over the years, and called it home, but often wondered how a city with so much rottenness could still be so beautiful. What kind of God—and he only marginally believed in God—would let some of the filth he witnessed each day perpetuate? It seemed like a monstrous contradiction; the same kind of contradiction inherent in the blessing of a country whose settlers slaughtered one race and then went on to enslave another. What kind of God would allow those things and then allow the oppressors of those other races to prosper? It did not seem to make sense. But America was rich and powerful, and San Francisco was beautiful and that was the way that it was. Those facts could not be denied.

Perhaps it was not for Grady to understand such discrepancies and apparent inequities. Perhaps people were meant to just accept their own personal lots and not think on large scales. That was true for Grady because thinking only about himself and his own survival and concerns was all that he, and many people like him, could handle. Thinking too far outside the box, so to speak, might cause such people to lose themselves and Grady banked a lot on his stability of action and thought.

Meanwhile though, thinking about Edward Chen was never too far from his mind. He continued to rationalize that he had been given a unique opportunity, an opportunity to respond to generations of oppression and he really didn't have to do anything, just keep his mouth shut about what he had seen. That might be revenge enough for him. As for San Francisco, it would probably always be beautiful and he was going to enjoy it as he walked.

His daughter re-entered his mind also as he walked and he was not one to forget specifics. His body might feel weak sometimes, but his mind was still sharp, and he was proud of that. He thought of the letter his daughter had slipped under his door, stating that she needed him to come to Hunter's Point this weekend. He did not like going over there, but he had to help her out if he could. She and his grandson were all that he had, and he and his daughter had been close when she was young. They had grown apart over her decisions not to go to college, despite performing well in high school, and over her choice of men. He also suspected that she might have drug problems, though she managed to conceal that. He would visit her this weekend, if for no other reason than to check on the status of his grandson Paul.

As he continued his walk, he saw his daughter's face reflected in the streets, for among the rich and well-off faces that he passed, there were also the faces of the desperate and the despairing, especially as he got closer to Market Street.

Market Street seemed to contain the embodiments of every stage of human development and consciousness within the span of five blocks. There were strip clubs across the street from five-star hotels, next door to souvenir shops and fast food chains. Those fast food shops were also across from chic cafes and high-priced bistros.

While navigating Market Street, one might have to step around or through vomit, human feces, and human beings sprawled on the sidewalks, or tourists reading guidebooks, bike messengers weaving through traffic, skateboarders, ex-hippies, and panhandling veterans. People spouted philosophy, played music, sold things, or just laid down and slept in plain sight. Public exposure in San Francisco was not uncommon, with someone urinating or squatting for a bowel movement, in broad daylight for all to see. Complete nakedness by some of the locals even happened from time to time. It was all part of the city's enduring legacy and charm of social freedom and exhibitionism.

San Francisco seemed to implicitly encourage this legacy since the early days of the Gold Rush, through the Beat and Hippie movements of the 1960s, all the way to the present, and all these types of behaviors always had the city government's tacit approval. Though Yuppies from throughout the nation had recently moved into the city in droves, they merely adapted to the city's free-spirited ways and did not complain about its sometimes-crude behaviors. To do so might violate the spirit they had come to the city to embrace. New York might be in the process of cleaning up Time Square, but for San Francisco to do so would be like tearing off an arm, going against its tradition of freedom and openness, which its leaders believed made it what it was. If Washington, D.C. was the head and brains of the nation, where the laws of the land were debated and created, then San Francisco was the loins, existing strictly for the pleasures of the flesh and sometimes the sacrifice of human order and decency.

Such a philosophy of living could manifest itself in some ugly ways, both physically and socially, and Grady got a full dose of the city's nasty, selfish side on his walk, as he found himself jostled and ignored by the mad hordes. While he wanted to keep up with the city, he felt that he might be getting too old to do so. Back in the 60s and 70s, he had been *a part of the scene,* but over the years, he had become a bit more conservative and resolved to be more of an observer of the glorious and the grotesque life around him.

He used to be able to objectively laugh at the city's idiosyncrasies and the things that made it what it was, but he felt himself becoming more judgmental with age. He did not always like what he was forced to look at, the dirty homeless or the shifty-eyed youths in doorways up to who knew what; but like most, he ignored what he saw, avoided eye contact with those who looked predatory and kept on moving, only observing the finer things to the eye, like the skies, the tall buildings under the clouds, the pretty young women here and there, the passing streetcars, and the wayward tourists. San Francisco still had him in its grasp, and only occasionally did he entertain the thought of leaving it.

"I'm gettin' old," he muttered to himself as he finally reached Market Street. "Too old for all these people and this nonsense."

He thought briefly about catching a bus to return home, but was not sure of the right one, since he had not taken one along this particular route in a while. He would have to make the return walk as best as he could.

When he got to the McDonald's, he expected to see Walter, Bill, and Wizard, his three coffee buddies. They might be found there around this time. Walter and Wizard were around his age; Bill, the white guy and ex-Hippie, was about 10 years younger. Walter was a black man with a grizzled beard, who showed up when he could scrape enough money together, either by panhandling, begging from relatives, or after his $317.00-a-month check from the city arrived. He and Bill were both sporadically homeless, living in the streets when they did not want to stay in shelters. As unstable as he acted and appeared, Wizard actually had a stable place to stay and sleep at night. It had something to do with relatives of his that helped to look out for him and take care of him. He had allowed San Francisco to affect his mental stability over the years, but he had never been able to leave. The city had him in its grip -- possibly for life.

Walter was a little darker skinned than Grady, with a round head and thinning, nappy hair. He always wore the same large greenish coat, no matter the temperature, and the city could run into the 90s on occasion. Walter had skinny legs and a large upper body that spoke of hard work at an early age, and he still carried around a southern accent that was so thick one could almost imagine the voices of slaves from an earlier time.

Originally from Louisiana, Walter told Grady that he had picked cotton as a boy to help his parents sharecrop. He had made his way out to California on a train because he said social conditions during his earlier days were rough. "Haad bein' a black man back den," he had told Grady and Grady had wholeheartedly understood. "Always hard being a black man in some kind a' way, though it's gotten a little better since those days, I spose," Grady had responded.

Bill was bald and had piercing blue eyes behind crumbling, round, black-framed glasses that he refused to upgrade. He had been in the city ever since the so-called *Summer of Love*. He liked telling stories of those days, and how San Francisco had never been the same since the yuppies moved in and took over the place. Bill was locked in a romantic San Francisco past, a slave himself also, despite his race. He did not want to leave San Francisco because he loved the city as much as the yuppies did. It had a hold on him as it had a hold on most people.

San Francisco could not get a hold on everyone, but if it did, it was hard to shake. A person would make all kinds of sacrifices just to remain there and to breathe the air. It had a magical, mystical, even supernatural quality to which many of the diehard residents did not even know they were subject. Grady had wondered over the years why San Francisco's Golden Gate Bridge had become such a key destination for suicide jumpers. He felt that there was something spooky and unusual about that, but his thoughts never lingered on it too much. For him, bridge suicides were just another manifestation of the city's *crazy* side.

Bill, meanwhile, had driven a taxi for a number of years, but the stiff competition among drivers and their companies easily weeded out the ones who could not produce substantially. Bill could not keep up because he was just not made that way: to be a hardcore capitalist. Like Grady, Bill had also lived in cheap apartment in the Tenderloin at one point, while he drove a cab, but lost his little room when he lost his ability to pay the rent. Now his breakfast, lunch, and dinner came from a local church pantry on Ellis Street and he received the same check each month from the city that Walter did.

Bill was great for stories about when he left Oregon as a teen, came to the city, partied for nearly a decade, saw hippies, rockers, bikers, protests, uprisings, concerts, mayors come and go, city councils, corruption, scandals, governors, religious cults, serial killers, assassinations, disco, sports teams, AIDS, gay revolutions, earthquakes, tremors, and the yuppie boom.

"San Francisco will never be the same," Grady remembered him saying once. "We stood for something back then. San Francisco, Berkeley, Oakland. Mario Savio, the Panthers. All the west coast; Ken Kesey, Janis Joplin, The Fillmore, the Airplane, and Bill Graham putting together the best shows ever seen. Now look at this crap. All these people care about is the flavor of their next cup of coffee. They got no heart. It's all a joke now."

Both he and Walter would make extra money panhandling, mostly on Market Street. When Grady arrived, they were both there sharing an outdoor table, drinking coffee, as the bustling world zoomed back and forth in front of them, so close they might be able to reach out and touch it; but, at this point in their lives, they were generally unable to keep up with the new world, and what it was becoming.

Wizard, the fourth member of their little group, was not there. Grady had met them all over the years, during his excursions to McDonald's, or taking breaks from his job.

Among this particular fast food establishment's latest innovations was the outdoor patio. Everything in the city, even McDonald's, was seeking to be posh and chic these days.

"Hey Jonas," Bill said when he saw Grady. "Pull up a chair. You must be off today. You didn't get fired did you? Then you would end up just like us." Both Bill and Walter roared with laughter at that statement.

"I been there before," Grady said. "I think I told ya'll that. Right after my wife died." They each remembered pieces and parts of Grady's life, which he had told them over time. He had once been married and lived in a house in the city's Sunset District. There, he raised his daughter and worked as a handyman around town. But when his wife died from cancer in 1978, he sold the house and got an apartment in the Haight District and lived off the home's sale.

Once Grady's money from the sale of the house ran out, he found it difficult to make ends meet by just being a basic repairman. Housing costs in the city also started to rise, and his apartment rent increased. As he struggled to find a job in the late 80s, he was eventually evicted from his Haight Street apartment. For a full month he found himself homeless in the city. It was a rough month of long days and cold nights. He had tried to forget it over the years. Still too young at that the time to collect social security, he answered an ad in the paper for a security guard position. He literally stumbled upon the ad in a two-day old newspaper he found in the street. The interview went well enough and he got the job.

What his friends didn't know was that he had to get cleaned up first to respond to the ad, so he moved in with his daughter to get himself together for the interview. After he got the job, he remained with his daughter for a while as he saved enough money to find a new place of his own. It was a long commute by bus every day from where his daughter lived to the San Francisco financial district, and he did not like his daughter's part of town, especially after dark. It also hurt his pride to be so dependent on her.

That was 1988, almost a full eight years ago. He still had not saved any money to speak of, because he was generally bad with money, but at least now he had a job and a place to live. Though he was not getting any younger, he had vowed never to let himself get into that position in life again.

"Be right back," he said, about to enter the Golden Arches to get a cup of coffee and something to eat. "Seen Wizard today?" he asked before he left.

"Maybe out dere sumwhere talkin' to hisself," Walter said. "He mite show up tuhday. Ya nevuh no wit him." Both Bill and Grady smiled before Grady went through the double doors to stand in line.

Wizard could be unbalanced, but at the present time, his behavior was benign. From time to time though, one might see him on Market Street, or even on one of the side streets, talking to himself in fact, or gesticulating wildly.

One day about two years ago, he had been out front of the building where Grady worked. Grady and Tony were at the desk and Big Eric was hanging out with them. All three saw him outside the doors in a dirty, dark overcoat with thick, uncombed hair, looking like some mad, black street prophet, who waved his hands in the air, and appeared to call on help from above.

Watching him that day and watching the reactions of the people walking by him on the sidewalk, the three men inside had different reactions. Not being able to help it because it was occurring at his work environment, Grady felt some shame and had only wanted Wizard to go away, to move on to the next block or back down to Market Street.

The brutish Eric, also feeling substantial embarrassment at a representative of his race performing in such a way for all the world to see, even went as far as to offer to go outside and move Wizard away from the building premises by force, suggesting at the time that he would be doing the police a favor.

Tony, younger and not really into the concept of race respectability, saw Wizard as just another madman, in a city where the people were free to rant and rave as they pleased. For Tony, Wizard was more a disgrace to professionalism and personal dignity and a blight on the building property. Tony had seen Wizard before as well and did not feel it was worth his effort at the moment to get rid of him. A modern black realist, Tony merely uttered with a casual shrug, "He'll be gone in a few minutes. The wind will come along and move him to the front of someone else's building. That's how it works out here."

Though he knew Tony was right, Grady was still torn by his own embarrassment over Wizard's behavior. For the reputation of his building and Wizard's own safety, he felt compelled to go out and talk to him. Also, Grady did not want to see his friend subjected to Eric's more violent measures. That might only make the situation worse.

What Grady remembered from that incident nearly two years ago, where he was able to go out and talk to Wizard briefly and usher him down the street, was the look in Wizard's eyes. They were clear, intelligent, and purposeful. He did not necessarily look "crazy"; he looked focused and determined. Today, however, Wizard was nowhere in sight and Grady still wanted to probe his thoughts on the Edward Chen incident. Though he was a part-time vagrant, Wizard was still the smartest black man that Grady knew.

After baby-stepping his way through the line, Grady returned to the patio table and got right to the point. "So did ya'll hear about that Chinese fella that was killed downtown last night?"

CHAPTER IX

But shortly after Grady had posed this question, the three of them witnessed a commotion up the street. About a block away, Grady, who was facing that direction, saw a dark figure in a dark over garment with arms outstretched so that the slack from his coat looked like wings. It looked like a black angel coming down the street parting the confused, and even frightened tourists, as he moved forward. Taking deliberate high steps, he also looked like an uncouth soldier in some foreign military parade.

It was Wizard, and as he made his way down the block, he comprised yet one more freakish attraction on San Francisco's now crowded Market Street. Slowing his pace down as he made his way down the block, he stopped at the three men's table, recognizing them.

"Afternoon gentlemen," he said, through a dignified voice that seemed to contradict his antics from just moments ago.

"What's going on, Wizard?" they responded in turn. Grady sometimes still experienced a twinge of shame when seen publicly with Wizard. He liked Wizard, thinking he was good for a few laughs and even some occasional insights, but he was not prepared to endorse *all* of Wizard's wild ways all the time, and at the moment, Wizard was looking pretty wild, both in general demeanor and in dress.

Nevertheless, Wizard vowed to return and join them after getting some coffee of his own. As for Bill, he had seen so much during his years in the city that his tolerance for anything, no matter how unusual, was always at a high level. Ever nostalgic for *old San Francisco,* Bill still valued eccentric behaviors over yuppie conformity any time. Of all of them, it was Bill who most believed Wizard's tale of having once been a professor at San Francisco State University in the early 1980s.

"Must be something in the air today," Bill said.

"He'll be all right," Grady said, "once he starts talkin'. That's what he wants to do. He wants somebody to talk to for a while. Everybody wants that."

"He all right," Walter nodded. "Wizard all right. Everybody in dis city crazy anyway. He jes anothuh won. He jus' one mo'?" He chuckled after saying this.

When Wizard returned, his demeanor had transformed somewhat. He crossed his legs and leaned back in his steel and rubber patio chair, assuming a kind of wise, professorial bearing that even people passing in the street could not help but notice. He looked to them like an intelligent black man with important things to say, almost like a modern-day Frederick Douglass with his broad, handsome face and thick, but nappy, swath of black and gray hair. In another time and space, he might have been someone of great importance. An older black man like themselves, Grady and Walter understood Wizard on a fundamental level.

As for his once being a college teacher, neither of them could say for sure. To Bill, Wizard was always worth a listen as long as he was calm, and Wizard also made Bill nostalgic for black intellectuals of a bygone era: men like Eldridge Cleaver, Stokely Carmichael, Huey Newton, H. Rap Brown, Malcolm X, and others. Ironically, Bill was more familiar with these men than either Grady or Walter. Though they knew that he was smart, Grady and Walter could relate best to Wizard the man, while Bill wanted to relate mostly to Wizard the cultural symbol and thinker.

"What brings you out today Wizard?" Grady asked, hoping to generate a discussion that would lead back to the question about the Edward Chen murder he had posed to Walter and Bill before Wizard had arrived.

"Gotta come out and look at this world at least once a day," Wizard responded. "The fabric of life is very fragile."

"Somethin' gon' happen?" Walter felt obliged to ask. "You know somethin' we don't?"

"No man can know everything. Truth is relative and it taunts us with its imprecision."

"Yea, there are always problems on the horizon," Bill offered lazily and cynically. "There were problems twenty years ago; there were problems ten years ago. And we still have problems now. The problem is people. Why did God create people? I'd like to ask him that one day. He could have just made nature and the animals and stopped right there. I think I would have done it that way."

"Now that is a philosophy!" Wizard responded excitedly, before taking a sip of coffee and contracting his body for greater warmth. The downtown winds could often blow their coldest on Market Street.

"But which God are you referring to my friend?" Wizard asked of Bill.

"The only God. The one true God," Bill responded with a defiance that even surprised himself. He had not expected to defend God today, but he could not help himself.

"Do you mean the God of the Bible? That must be what you mean, as an American. Is that correct?" Wizard asked, with a tone of condescension in his voice.

"That's the one," Bill responded through a sarcasm that came natural to him. "The God that is up there watching us all right now. He is watching us sitting here right now, drinking coffee, and talking about him."

"Hahahaha!!!" Wizard laughed out so loud that passersby looked over at him from the sidewalk. "Next you are going to tell me about all that Heaven and Hell business," he added through a freshly mocking tone.

"Well I don't know about all that," Bill confessed as Grady and Walter looked on and listened, with only marginal interest. "I haven't gone over the details in a long time. But in my gut I believe there is a God who is in control of everything, and just one God at that. I don't believe in the *many Gods* theory. That doesn't make sense to me and the Bible is the key to all of it. My mind might be messed up from all my partyin' years, but do I remember what I learned when I was a kid."

"And what do you believe gentleman, might I ask?" Wizard said, now directing his attention to Grady and Walter.

"I buhlieve in Gawd," Walter acknowledged first. "Uh grew up in the chuch back in Lisiana. Uh'll always buhlieve in Gawd, uh suppose. Ha else did we git heah? Whu'd uhl dis come frum?"

Grady had been listening, but had not anticipated a discussion of religion today either, and he wanted to divert it to conversation about what had happened to him the other night.

His own belief in God was more deistic: that though there might have been a force responsible for creating everything, that being's interaction in human affairs was now limited. How man handled his affairs was now up to him after birth and how he behaved in life would determine what happened upon death. A God of some kind would determine that on some kind of ledger sheet when all was said and done, but man's fate while on earth was in his own hands.

"We can talk about this another time," Grady jumped in after Walter, because he wanted some answers or some advice, and he could not hang around all day. "Before you came up we was talkin' about that Chinese fella that that was killed the other night."

Unfortunately for him, none of them knew what he was talking about because they had not followed the recent news.

"You mintined dat. But uh ain't heard nuttin' about it," Walter said.

"Me neither," Bill said.

A bit flustered, Grady replied: "I was curious 'cause it happened aroun' the corner from my buildin' and I saw it on the news. They still don't know who is responsible."

"I do not own a television set and I rarely read the newspapers," Wizard interjected. "Too much propaganda. If need information, I go to the public library and I only read the books."

"As for that belief in that God of yours," Wizard directed specifically at Bill, "the world is moving to a post-God culture. Whether you believe in God or not is irrelevant and human faith is inconsequential. Material reality, human nature, and human will are all that matter. They are all that will matter in the future, regardless of the past."

Bill liked Wizard but he did not feel like getting into a debate with him today, and not in a religious debate either. "Let Jonas here talk" he said. "He's obviously got something to say about something."

"Did ya see sumthin'? Do ya know sumthin'," Walter added about the incident that Grady had mentioned. "Is dat wuh ya askin' fo'?"

Grady was briefly shaken and made to feel slightly paranoid by the question and the sudden focus on him and his concerns.

"Nah," he said, attempting to sound calm and nonchalant about the matter. He was also frustrated with their ignorance over the Chen incident, which had already been publicized. "I only wanted to know if ya'll had heard about it. It was all over the news." And then he remembered the newspaper that was now face down on the outdoor table. "Here," he said, showing them Edward Chen's picture on the front page.

"Must be important for him to be on the front page," Wizard offered, "and Chinese at that. Except for the street gangs back in the 70s, Asians in this city stay away from violent crime, either as victims or perpetrators. But just from the placement on the front page, I can tell this is important. He must have been someone with some clout, as they say."

"What's the story, Jonas?" Bill asked suspiciously. "Why are you showing us all this? Do you know something about it or not?"

All of a sudden, Grady started to feel pinned to a wall because he might have tipped his hand by presenting too much information. But if he divulged everything that he knew to them, he might as well go directly to the police right afterwards, because the secret would be out and he was not ready to give it up yet. All he wanted from them right now was to know how they might have reacted in his situation, but he was having difficulty steering them in that direction. Perhaps it was better if he left or dropped the subject altogether.

"I don't know nothin' about it, like I said," Grady said, responding to Bill's near miss question. "I was workin' but I had already gone home. I heard some sirens around midnight. Thas about it. Then I heard something about it on the news this morning. But I gotta go. I'll be workin' my regular shift tomorrow and probably see you fools again during my lunch break."

They all gave a collective "goodbye" as Grady merged himself back into the Market Street foot traffic. He had gotten nothing out of them to aid in his dilemma. Perhaps it had been his approach. He had tried to be as subtle as possible, but he could not blame them for their ignorance of the situation. This was his problem to solve, not theirs. In all, he had hung out with his friends for about 30 minutes.

While walking, he thought seriously about going to a police station before he went home but was not sure what he would say when he got there. He would be offering late information and the longer he waited the guiltier *he* would look, as he would be asked what took him so long to come forward; and might they not give him even more trouble because he was black?

Society had less mercy and forgiveness for black people, he had learned over the years. Blacks had to be perfect and the best of the best citizens, with little or no margin for error at all times it seemed. He had learned this growing up, sometimes painfully, in the South. Even if they came across as perfect and doing the right thing, that was sometimes not even good enough. No, at this point, he would wait it out and continue to see how the incident played out in the media. In fact, he might never have to come forward at all. Something else might happen before then. It was still his choice.

On the way home, he remembered to buy some light bulbs to finally replace the one out in his hallway. But when he got home and screwed a new one in, it still fizzled and flickered, apparently due to a wiring problem. Unfortunately, McTeague had not been there when he entered the building and he remained stuck with four new bulbs and a still-dying light.

Later that evening, Grady learned new revelations about the Chen case. For the first time, the police, through the media, were speculating that Edward Chen had, in fact, been murdered. Fibers of Chen's hair had been found in a spot on the wall above where his body had been found.

"What took 'em so long to decide dat?" Grady muttered to himself on his sofa, as a cool wind blew in through his window. He sat watching the news, finishing off the last of the wine as the light thinned inside his apartment, overwhelmed by the approaching dusk.

More information on Chen's life was also given. His wife again appeared on the screen, only this time she did not try to fight back tears. She asked for help from anyone who might have seen what happened to her husband. Her hair was jet black, about shoulder length, and as she sobbed it swung in and out of her face and eyes like wiper blades. Grady believed her tears were real and believed the woman was in pain; nevertheless, he remained unmoved by her plea. Grady had seen suffering from personal loss before and it was a part of life. He believed that suffering was universal, even for Asians; and though he understood the woman's pain, it was not sympathy he felt for her, but curiosity and some mild contempt.

"I seen women cry befo'," he spoke heatedly toward the television, the wine now having some effect on his behavior and emotions. "Black women! You ain't no different. And what that white man did to yo' husband, he'll get his one day. Don't you worry. But it ain't gon' come from me!"

As it turned out, the Chen family had somewhat of a small empire in local real estate, owning some 30 large properties in San Francisco and Daly City. They had money and ties that went all the way to Hong Kong, the media reported. Regardless of what the police said, the media was basically saying that a murder had taken place in the heart of San Francisco's financial district.

People interviewed in the street and a couple of city council members all said that an answer must be found for the sake of preserving "civility" in San Francisco society. But though there continued to be much speculation, no one, not even the police, seemed to be able to put forward a possible scenario as to what could have specifically happened.

The media, meanwhile, also continued to build on the pathos resulting from Chen's death. Chen had played lacrosse at St. Ignatius High School, one of the few Asians in the history of the school to start on the varsity team. He had graduated *summa cum laude* from Berkeley in economics and had graduated near the top of his class from business school.

Someone Grady had never heard of two days earlier was now a kind of local celebrity. Chen's story had nearly supplanted Arthur Grant's over in Oakland. Grant was a victim; Chen was becoming a posthumous hero. There was something wrong with that disparity in Grady's mind. The stories being told were not equal, not fair, and Grady was getting the chance to compare them up close. "The Chinese man bein' glorified in his death," Grady snorted somewhat drunkenly.

Arthur Grant's death had not garnered quite as much attention, and his life seemed to have garnered none at all, in comparison. Grant had not accomplished much by some standards. He had had a small prison record, a job at warehouse, and a child for whom he had tried to provide. To the media, this could not stack up next to Chen's accomplishments in the world. From Grady's perspective, it seemed as if Grant was just another black man who had a bad run in with the law.

The latest in the Grant case, which the news also reported that evening, was that anger and resentment were still brewing in Oakland over Grant's shooting. Elements of the public wanted the white police officer arrested and tried for murder. There would be protests tomorrow at the site of the shooting.

"That's right," Grady said to himself, with wine glass still in hand. "They need to get that cracker. I might go over there and protest myself." He laughed wryly at this consideration, but recording the disparities between the two cases hardened Grady even more against providing any information to aid the investigation into Chen's death.

When the news was over, Grady prepared his uniform for work the next day, and made ready for bed. He closed his window this time though, feeling indescribably paranoid tonight and not wanting the San Francisco air to exacerbate that feeling.

In the morning, the news regarding Chen's death changed again. The police, and not the media, were now definitely calling the death a homicide. This was based on further evidence collected at the scene. The news reported that they were perhaps looking for someone that Chen did not know and might have bumped into that night. They were even going as far as to classify the incident as a possible example of "Street Rage," based on the information that Chen had no known enemies, that he was on a routine errand, the fact that nothing had been taken from his person, and the nature of his injuries. The police suggested the way the crime might have even been committed, employing theories so closely parallel to what had actually happened, that it sent a chill down Grady's spine, as he watched the morning broadcast. In a short amount of time they had now laid out what had happened with near complete accuracy.

But the effect of the new information created even more distance between Grady and the crime. To him, the police were doing exactly what they were paid to do, so now there was even less reason for him to get involved. Yet, Grady couldn't stop going over it in his head. Arthur Grant over in Oakland, and black people in general, got no justice at all. The justice in Chen's case experienced only a slight delay. He again marveled at the speed with which the authorities pursued the apparent murder of *one of their own*. Grady was sure that if a black man had been killed in the financial section of the city, he would not get the same treatment.

Still, he found himself stunned, overwhelmed, and even impressed by law enforcement's abilities. The news reporter reconstructed a possible scenario that police investigators had related to him, where one, or even possibly two people might have approached Chen for some reason, an argument or altercation might have ensued, followed by a struggle, and then Chen was slammed into the side of the building.

Knowing that this was almost exactly what happened, Grady could not help but be intrigued by the very drama of what might happen next. There was even talk, for the first time, of a possible reward, with more information to come from the family later.

With all these new revelations in his head, Grady headed for work, to the environment that had produced Edward Chen, and possibly the killer as well. Grady still had not given much thought to the killer. It was as if he felt protected from that criminal and had to think about him only when and if he pleased. But what if the man killed again? If the man were to do that, then the police would have another crime to solve, though he did not think the man to be some kind of a serial killer. The crime appeared to Grady to be just as the police had speculated, one of opportunity, or even an accident. Two guys got into something on a street corner that turned tragic. What the perpetrator of the crime was doing right now was of little concern to Grady. For him, his overall indifference was part of the same equation. He could not afford to care about either violator or victim because one could influence the other in his heart. In other words, if he caved in and showed weakness to shed light on the case in one area, he would have to do so overall.

As he walked to work though, he could not help but think about the killer again. The man was getting away with murder, was he not? Grady could justify his own actions and the workings of his own conscience in this case, but what kind of conscience did this man have? He had killed someone and must have known it by now. The idea of the human conscience was important here, but did not this man have much more to confess than Grady?

When he got to work, Grady found himself looking at the people who occupied the building now in a different light. He used to hold them in some esteem, but now their value had diminished. They were to him now as vicious, savage, and brutal as the people over in the Hunter's Point section of the city were often portrayed. The people in his building offered him nothing anymore, if they ever did.

Grady was working with Tony this day. Tony was in charge of the guards and he always told the guards who worked for him that they were there to serve and protect the interests of the tenants and the building. Grady was not so sure of his overall loyalty and support anymore, in light of recent events. He was, however, careful not to show that anything was wrong. Overall, he was not sure anymore where his loyalties laid.

Grady's return to work turned out to be overall uneventful. He kept what was inside him to himself, did his job, and waited for the day to end. On his break at McDonald's, he did not see any of his friends as he thought he might. This was good, because he did not feel like talking a lot today anyway.

CHAPTER X

When he got home for the day, the bulb in the hallway still flickered. The flickering bulb appeared like a beacon, or maybe even some kind of coded warning. It was like it was sucking on its last breath. McTeague was nowhere to be found again. Grady might have to call the building owner to get the light fixture repaired, or maybe he would talk to Spike about it. Spike, appearances notwithstanding, was the most responsible tenant in the building. He made sure to get things done, even if it meant doing them himself.

Grady had not seen Spike in a couple of weeks, but he would check with him on Saturday morning before going go see his daughter and grandson. There was welcome silence in the hall and above his head, meanwhile. The silence meant that Lorraine was at the food pantry where she worked and the Hispanic family had yet to get home. Grady would enjoy what afternoon quiet he would be afforded.

But as soon as he got inside his apartment, away from the flickering light in the hallway, Grady immediately heard the door open at Lorraine's apartment, some voices, the door closing again, and then someone who did not head toward the exit of the building, but upstairs instead. Since Grady knew that the

Hispanic family was currently the only occupant of the entire third floor, he thought this a little unusual.

He tried to keep out of the business of others, but Tenderloin apartment life was close quarters and one would be a fool not to be always aware of one's surroundings and the comings and goings of others. Grady gave no more thought to this unusual circumstance at the moment because he wanted to watch the evening news for any information on what might be going on with the Chen murder. Right now, he was consumed with being a theater participant where the case was concerned. He also continued to like the power he had as still being the only apparent witness to the crime.

Meanwhile there were, in fact, new developments in the case. Not only was there now a $50,000 reward, but there seemed to be a potential suspect. It turned out that someone had seen something from across the street, but had only now come forward to give his information. The police did not show his face on camera, but the unidentified man had told them that he had seen the figure of an African-American man over Chen's body as it lay at the corner, though he had been unable to come up with details other than that.

The reward had been issued by Jennifer Chen herself, Edward Chen's wife. The money would be given to anyone providing information leading to the arrest and conviction of her husband's killer. The police still maintained that they had no suspects, but indicated that they were now looking for a tall black man in dark clothing. Offended by this new information at first, Grady was forced to confront a stark revelation.

"But they lookin' for the wrong man," he said to himself, simultaneously confused and angry. "He won't black. He was white." And then it dawned on him. "And that means they could be lookin' for me."

A strong urge to correct this wrong came over him and he could not resist it. He immediately called the police department. He would not reveal all the information that he knew, but he felt he at least had to set some information straight.

"He wasn't black, he was white," he told someone at the end of the phone, after getting through on a police line and telling the operator that he had some information about the murder of Edward Chen.

"Excuse me, sir?" the officer said to the angered Grady. "Who is this?"

"The killer is why I am callin'" Grady said. "That killer was white. That's all I kin tell you. So, you all don't need to waste your time searchin' for no black man. Enough of them in jail already." After saying this, Grady hung up the phone before the person on the other end could respond.

He needed some air after the call and opened his window. He felt better because he had corrected a potential wrong and he had gotten something off his conscience at the same time. It had been building there and now he felt that he had given something back, though there was much more information that he *had not* given. He wanted to keep this to himself until he felt the time was right. He still wanted to see what the police could come up with on their own. *Let them do their jobs,* he continued to think.

But he also thought about the reward that was now being offered. He had not gotten into this thing because of greed. But now that a possible reward was on the table, he wondered if he could not somehow profit from it. After all, he was still, to his knowledge, the only one who could solve the case, and money was always welcome, though he tended to be a poor manager of it. He might also be able to share some of the money with his daughter and grandson.

It was remarkable, Grady considered, standing and looking out of his window, down the alley, and into the early evening street, that he had been the only apparent witness to the crime and the only person to get a good look at the killer up close. What a small window of experience and time! Like a finger of God was directed from the heavens specifically at him in some sort of a test of conscience. *What are you going to do, and why?* a voice was seeming to say.

At 65, there was not much time left for Grady on planet Earth. Health-wise, he was starting to feel short of breath and he was not able to walk as far as in the past. He did not know the cause of this, but knew that old age had to be a part of it. He was not at all overweight and had stopped smoking years earlier.

He did not like doctors and usually only went in cases of absolute emergency, like when an ambulance had to be called. He never went for preventative measures. He was stubborn that way.

So maybe witnessing this murder was some sort of test before death. Or maybe it was a chance to earn some money through the reward. What could he do with the reward money, anyway?

He could move. He could save some. He could help out his daughter and grandson. He would have to think about this and think about it fast. Where money was involved, time was short.

The next day at work was again uneventful for the most part, except for the usual Friday busyness. At the heart of it was that everyone in the city was looking forward to the weekend and the general revved-up activity always seemed to be in anticipation of this.

The lobby was busy all morning with steady flows of foot traffic, and some people took the opportunity to leave early at various points of the day. Grady's Friday afternoon passed smoothly, where even Buddy behaved by doing his assignments and being and doing what was required of him. On this day, Buddy proved the theory to Grady that even the most lowdown and inept can be competent and thoughtful on a given day. But these thoughts were only fleeting as Grady's perspective on human nature, born in the racist South nearly a half century earlier, continued to be negative and dark in general. He knew that Buddy would stumble again eventually.

After a decent sleep Friday night, it was Saturday morning and he was ready to go see his daughter and grandson. There had been no new news in the Chen case overnight and Grady thought that he would get a paper and see if there was anything there. He would read it on the bus.

Before leaving his building, he stopped by to see Spike, who lived near the first-floor exit. When he knocked on Spike's door, he was only greeted by music that again sounded like a destructive apocalypse. Spike had once told Grady that he had been a Hell's Angel biker who cruised the California highways and lived a somewhat dangerous lifestyle. Even now he looked the part, with tattoos, earrings, muscular biceps, a beard, and a balding head. He looked like a tough guy, but he and Grady had always gotten along well. This was because he and Grady represented extremes in some ways: an experienced and aging black man and a biker tough guy in a city growing full of "yuppie" types, with whom neither of them could really relate.

Grady and Spike each lived on society's margins in many ways and they bonded over that. Despite their differences, there was also an unspoken father-son relationship that neither of them acknowledged, but nevertheless appreciated. Grady had given Spike advice in the past and Spike had accepted it. Aside from that, Spike had a playful way about him and was one of those people that the mantra "you can't judge a book by its cover" seemed to describe. Simply put, he was not as scary as he appeared, but he was tough, and he did have some redeeming abilities, as all people did.

Right now though, Grady could not even guess what kinds of instruments were used to play the music that was coming from Spike's apartment. All Grady knew was that it was a long way from the jazz and blues that he could still locate on the radio occasionally. "That boy probably can't even hear me," Grady said to himself after knocking on Spike's door several times.

Grady also liked Spike because Spike was straightforward. In Grady's mind, people did not need to talk half as much as they did in life anyway.

Today, however, Spike was somewhere buried in his music and Grady would have to talk to him later about the building and its affairs.

The music though left a chilling impression on Grady as he left Spike's door. He wondered how someone could listen to that kind of assault on the ears for so long, up so close, and live to tell about it. To Grady's 65-year-old ears, it again sounded like the end of the world and he was relieved to leave it behind, to be replaced by the still-soothing sounds of the street.

❦

To see his daughter and grandson, Grady had to take the number 15 Third Street bus to the Bayview-Hunter's Point section of the city. After getting on the bus, he opened the newspaper he had purchased to get the latest on the case.

Overnight, despite what the television had said, the reward money had been increased from $50,000 to $100,000, due to a donation from the city's powerful Chinese Chamber of Commerce. There was also some dispute over the identity of the suspect, or even if there was one. Grady read this as his bus rattled its way down Larkin Street.

The headline ran: ***Reward Increased in Alleged Murder; Identity of Potential Suspect Disputed***

The identity of a possible suspect in the so-called San Francisco "Street Rage" killing is being disputed by police officials, while the reward for information leading to an arrest and conviction in the death of real estate developer Edward Chen has been doubled.

Police officials would not confirm or deny that they received an anonymous call indicating that the alleged killer was a Caucasian male. The call was made apparently to dispute the latest information wherein a witness had reported seeing a black man over the body the night it was found.

An unnamed police official reported to this newspaper that a precinct officer had received a tip from an unidentified caller claiming to be in the vicinity of the crime that night. The caller, the official said, apparently had called to "set the record straight" but had not been willing to reveal any further information about what he knew.

"The caller seemed to be a little agitated," the official said. "But that's about the extent of it." Asked if there was any way to reach the caller or if the information given might alter the focus of the investigation, the officer would only say that "the department and the homicide division are investigating all leads and considering all possibilities."

Meanwhile, SFPD spokesman Kirby Lockett, speaking for the department on the record, said that he had no information about such a call, but that he and his staff would look into it. He added that it was the SFPD's responsibility to conduct as full an investigation as possible.

Yesterday meanwhile, the San Francisco Chinese Chamber of Commerce and several other prominent local Chinese organizations, volunteered to increase the reward money for information in the death of Edward Chen to $100,000 from the $50,000 already offered by the victim's family.

"He was a son of the city, with a long rich history of citizenship and service to the city and county of San Francisco," Commerce chairman Marvin Yee said of Chen. "He represented his family and the Chinese community well. We owe it to him to help bring closure to his death.

"Based on his family's legacy, he was China. He still spoke the language, which for many young Chinese is increasingly rare. He studied in Beijing briefly while he was in college to get a better sense of his heritage."

Yee said that he was certain that whoever was responsible would be found, though he would not comment on the new information concerning the identity of any suspect.

"I have no comment on that. I only know what I hear
from the police and seek to have justice enacted as swiftly
as possible."

Grady folded the paper in half as his bus climbed a hill. The nature of the passengers had changed quickly and dramatically after he had crossed Market Street and he felt that he had to keep his wits about him more.

Hunter's Point, the hub of black life in San Francisco, also had the highest crime rate, and now he was going into the heart of it. This is where his daughter had chosen to live. Though it was still daytime, he still felt the need to be more alert than usual. He generally felt comfortable around black people, but he was also aware of their dark side.

He had experienced that in the South growing up and elsewhere in his life. Black people often lived in a kind of desperation and their frustrations could often affect others, especially their own kind, often violently.

Overall, he might be on the bus for another 20 minutes. As he rode, he noticed the kind of people getting on and off the bus, mostly blacks—young men and women, and some elderly. He eyed them quietly, as they did him, but he also thought anew about the reward and its increase.

Why shouldn't he make some money off this thing, at this point? He had not committed a crime. He had only the opportunity of witnessing it, and if asked why he had taken so long to say anything, he might only say that he was afraid of potential consequences, where he thought he might be victimized in some way at this point. No one could argue with that. He could also just say he was scared.

He would think about the reward more, while continuing to watch the case progress through the media. It was clear to him from today's article that the police knew little more than they knew from the start. In fact, they now seemed confused by new information that they did not understand. Therefore, barring that Chen's killer decided to make a confession, Grady, for lack of a better term, still "held all the cards," with the life of a white man in one hand and a grieving Chinese community in the other. The seductive feelings of power and influence over the situation still held him in their grip. Now the potential for double the reward was stirred into the mix. Was this a dangerous combination?

At the end of his ride, the bus stopped at the bottom of a hill about two blocks from where Grady knew he was going, and everybody started to unload. Grady got up too and went to the driver.

"I thought you went to the top of the hill," he said.

"We stopped about six months ago," the driver said. "This the end of the line. People walk it from here."

Feeling put out over this situation, Grady quickly realized he would have to walk the two blocks uphill to get to his daughter's apartment.

When he looked out through the bus's front window, Grady saw several of the youth who were on the bus with him, making their way up the hill, with an elderly woman moving slowly behind them. Seeing this angered Grady, but he had no choice but to get off the bus and start making his way up the hill too.

The Hunter's Point area was located in San Francisco's southeast corner. Some of it, the part where Grady was going to see his daughter, was situated on a collection of hills. It was comprised of groupings of white, townhouse-like tenements. The area's reputation in the city notwithstanding, it possessed what many locations near the water did: a stunning view of the San Francisco Bay and lands in the distance.

It was like a visual oxymoron: poverty and crime-stricken projects overlooking scenic vistas. Grady had been over here many times during his years in the city, though he had never wanted to live here. For one thing, it was too far from the places he needed to be.

The last time he was here was about eight months ago when he saw his daughter and grandson just for a visit. So, he was not a complete stranger to this part of town and knew some of the territory. He knew that his daughter lived at the back of a parking lot on the first-floor level. Her place was not what could be called "nice"; in fact, Grady thought it was a little worse than his own apartment in the Tenderloin, but it was somewhere to live.

While laboring to walk up the hill and trying to catch his breath, he managed to think about the reward money again. Surely, if he got it, he might be able to provide a little relief for the only family members he had. His ability to think about the money at this moment was clear proof that money considerations could even transcend physical fatigue, which he was experiencing.

As he approached the foot of the second and final block, he had to stop and rest. He found himself struggling to breathe. Having never had this problem so severely before, he started to wonder again about his overall health. Perhaps it might be time to get a checkup soon. He reminded himself that he had not had one in a while. He knew that he was getting older, but he did not believe he was actually in decline.

Helping his situation, however, was that it was a beautiful day, with light cool breezes and sunny skies. This made it hard to believe that he was standing in the so-called "worst" part of San Francisco. Then, as he started to resume his walk, he was quickly reminded of where he was when he saw a group of young men, in their teens and dressed in all black, rumbling down the sidewalk in his direction.

They were talking loudly and gesticulating, their largely unintelligible conversation laced with profanity. They looked at him with contemptuous eyes, though Grady, even at his age, knew that he had to hold his ground where eye contact was concerned. It was important in an environment like this that he did not show weakness.

As they glared at him, one of them intentionally brushed him as they walked by, in a form of intimidation. Grady absorbed the contact and stared back at the young black men proudly and defiantly, but with some deference. He wanted to let them know that he could not be intimated, but also that he was a visitor and did not want to presume too much on what was their *turf.* This technique worked and he resumed his climb, reaching the top of the hill, where he took the time to take another rest.

Looking back after the young men, who were now talking at bottom of the hill, Grady could not help but be a little envious of their youth and energy, and the way youths could traverse such physical obstacles like the hills in this area with such ease. They did not even think about it.

"Those days are over for me," he thought to himself and then he turned and walked in search of the opening to his daughter's parking lot. There were no more people in sight before him, as it was still relatively early on a Saturday morning.

As he continued this more leisurely walk, now devoid of any hills, Grady could not help but compare the present environment with the one he lived in and around. It was a tale of two cities. It was still San Francisco, but this was deprived San Francisco, wanting San Francisco, caged San Francisco, as opposed to the liberated, elaborate, ornate, Byzantine one on his side of the city.

This was black San Francisco, the city's own personal ghetto, and—looking at the buildings with their chipped paint, the cracked concrete sidewalks, the sparse foliage, and the impersonal architecture—Grady thought to himself about what the place must be like at night these days. He heard about the shootings over here, but had not been here during nighttime in a while.

It must be a nightmare, he thought, thinking that he knew black people, and how cruel they could be to one another. It was in the newspaper everyday: the shootings, the complaints of lack of services, the broken families, and the poor schools. It had to be much worse at night. "Yep, I bet some of 'em only come out at night," acknowledging to himself again the absence of people out on such a beautiful Saturday morning.

Rounding into his daughter's parking lot, Grady still saw no faces, no life, no human activity, not even a squirrel. The only people he had seen so far were the young toughs, who were headed in the opposite direction. He now found himself wondering where they were going so early. But images of them were quickly eclipsed by the breathtaking views just beyond the rooftop of his daughter's apartment. In the distance to the left one could see the Bay Bridge; to the center, directly across the bay, one could get a faint image of downtown Oakland's skyline; to the right was another breathtaking watery expanse of the San Francisco Bay itself.

Grady did not have such views from where he lived downtown, but doubted whether he would be able to appreciate what nature he saw now if he actually lived in Hunter's Point. There were always so many real-world distractions with which to contend.

His daughter's parking lot was full of cars and all of his daughter's neighbors appeared to be at home. They were all asleep it seemed. Grady knew that San Francisco could be a lazy city, especially on weekend mornings. He might have been asleep himself right now, if he was not on his present errand of mercy.

Neighborhood notwithstanding, some of the cars here were nice ones. He saw luxury cars and SUVs, all reflecting the sunlight. There were also some old junkers that screamed to be towed away. The presence of the nice cars in such a neighborhood was another *non-sequitur*. Grady looked at the scene believing that these people, his people, were doing nicer than their homes appeared. Then he rethought quickly.

"Some of it could be drug money," he muttered to himself judgmentally. "I know that." Having caught his breath now completely, he approached his daughter's door.

The last time he was here, the front of her apartment did not look as rundown as it did today. Today, the paint was worn, the screens were slashed or dangled from windows, and there was scattered trash around the doorstep.

After knocking loudly, he heard the sound of a television. He knocked loudly again to get above the set's volume. Soon, the door swung open and a black boy about age six or seven appeared, looking sleepy. He was wearing yellow pajamas with little red bears on them, but the outfit looked crusted and stained with food.

"Paulie," Grady asked. "How you doin' boy?"

The boy said nothing and only stared at Grady at first, his little hand wiping the sleep from his eyes.

"It's your granddaddy—remember?"

Absently, the boy looked again at Grady before speaking.

"Hi granddaddy," he said, and Grady pushed himself inside. Grady's daughter, Ruth, was not in sight, while the television was on and set to cartoons.

"Where's your momma?" Grady asked his grandson, who had grown a bit, but had not changed much otherwise, since Grady had last seen him.

"She sleep," Paulie responded.

"Sleep? Didn't she know I was comin'? I thought this was important to her."

Paulie, who had returned to his place on the floor in front of the television, said nothing.

The apartment was in mild disarray. The carpets were worn, some sofa cushions were on the floor and there was a stale smell in the air. Grady had heard that apartments in this area had trouble with mold and people reacting allergically to it. His daughter had never reported any of this to him concerning her apartment, but there had been some severe cases in the Bayview in recent years. People literally had trouble with day-to-day breathing in their own homes. Some were ultimately forced to move.

Grady left his grandson to return to his cartoons while he himself walked back to the bedroom to peek in on his daughter. He felt comfortable doing this. She was still family.

What he saw when he looked into the room and onto the bed were two black bodies, each tangled up in the covers. Neither was moving. The man with his daughter must be a new boyfriend, Grady thought. Grady turned from the room and walked back over to his grandson.

"Who's that in there with her?" he asked. Paulie, still on the floor and on his stomach, did not turn his eyes from the cartoon images.

"Das Chuck."

"Chuck?" Grady repeated unconsciously.

Paulie said nothing more, continuing to look at the screen.

"Well ok," Grady said. "You get up and go in there and tell her I'm here. She supposed to be up by now. We got somethin' to do and I can't stay here all day."

Paulie sprung up with energy he had not yet exhibited, as if he had been inspired by being sent on a mission. He was a happy messenger. In fact, he was happy to see his grandfather in general. He just didn't know how to express himself clearly. Like many children, he sometimes needed external instigation to communicate.

Without uttering a word, the young black boy followed instructions from the older man. Grady, meanwhile, looked around the apartment again. It was large—larger than his, in fact. The funny thing about black ghetto apartments was that they were often nice, in and of themselves. It was what was often done to them by their inhabitants that was the problem. Despite this, there was always plenty of square footage for decent and low prices. The highest "price" to be paid was always the price of living amongst one's own kind and the contempt that tended to breed. From Grady's experience over the years, black people often had a problem getting along when they got lumped together. It wasn't as bad back in the South when Grady was growing up years ago. But city life seemed to bring out the worst in black people.

Ten minutes later, Grady's daughter walked out from her bedroom. She went immediately to the refrigerator. She pulled out a soda without offering anything to Grady.

She was about 40 now. She had Paulie later in life, and by "mistake," after surgery on a fertility problem had supposedly not succeeded. She did not regret Paulie now even though his father was now absent. She only regretted that she could not do more for him. In general, she was depressed and often took it out through drugs and men.

"Let me get dressed," she said to her father. "That office won't be open for another half hour."

Ruth Jonas maintained a solid, lean frame, unlike a great many impoverished African American women who tended to gain substantial weight as they aged, and fought obesity. She was also quite intelligent. She just lived in a city that did not necessarily value such characteristics when they came from people of her race, particularly non-ambitious ones.

Essentially, Ruth had the same body she had 20 years earlier and it allowed her to do more, though she remained unemployed. She had experimented with crack and other drugs. She had been strong enough to fight them off, though temptations were always there in many other forms. Ruth possessed the same strong, southern constitution that her parents did, but her strength was waning. Like her father, she too was feeling the physical and emotional stress of daily life and trying to fight off the rage and contempt that often accompanied it.

Grady relaxed, now knowing that he would have to wait a little while for his daughter to get ready. He wanted to ask his daughter about the man in her room but did not feel like it was his place. She would tell him if she wanted.

The boy had come back and joined his grandfather, while the mother returned to her room to get prepared for her day. Within a half hour, she was back also. The apparent *boyfriend* stayed in the room. This was fine with Grady, as he had only expected to see his daughter and grandson today anyway, and he did not have the energy right now to evaluate the character of one of his daughter's suitors. He felt he might be disappointed by what he learned about the young man anyway.

While waiting for his daughter, Grady found that he had little to say to the child, other than asking him about school and health matters. The child only gave short, curt answers in response. The problem was that Grady did not spend enough time with his family, to have any regular conversations. He did not really know what to discuss with them because he was largely unaware of what was happening in their lives. Some of this stemmed from disputes the father and daughter had had over the years; they were also somewhat estranged because of Grady's general disdain for his daughter's side of the city. Grady generally did not like "ghetto" black people. He thought his daughter was too good for this environment, but here is where her life circumstances had led her.

"Ain't the boy coming with us?" Grady said, noticing that his grandson was not attempting to change his wardrobe.

"There's no reason for him to go," Ruth responded sharply. "All you have to do is sign a paper again. Just like last time."

"I understand that," Grady responded sharply, a cantankerous side of himself being stirred up, in a way that only a family member could provoke it. "I was thinking that we could spend a little time over heah before I go back. Aftah all, I did come

all the way over heah again. How do we get down to the water?
I don't remember."

All of a sudden, he was in no hurry to get back to his side
of San Francisco. He realized that he did not have much to do
today, and that he did not often get to see the water where he
lived. He had an overwhelming desire to see nature.

"There are some stairs behind here. I guess we can go down
there after we leave the office, if that girl is even there. You can't
depend on nobody these days to be where you want 'em and to
be on time." She lit a cigarette.

There was a brief pause in the conversation before Grady
spoke again: "That's a long walk up that hill," he said, expecting
a little sympathy for what his lungs and legs had to put up with
a half hour ago. Paulie was back in front of the television, but
now that his mother was in the room, he would turn around
occasionally and watch the adults.

"This city don't care nothin' about us over here," his daughter
responded flatly and abruptly to what Grady had said. "They
stopped that bus because they only want to give black people
the basic services. They hate us at City Hall and think they
can treat us any way they want, just because we're black. They
think we are just a bunch of good-for-nothing niggers over
here. We complain about this stuff to the board of supervisors,
but nothing ever gets done. They just think all black people
are a joke, stupid, and not worth paying attention to over here.
That's why there's so much killing over here, because these
people know they are hated by everybody, so we hate each
other. It's like that for black people everywhere." She then took
a drag from her cigarette, while standing with her back to her
refrigerator. "But I guess we all have to live somewhere."

Grady had not heard such fierce tones come from his daughter in a while. He knew she was capable of such deep thought, but right now she was more strident and militant than ever.

"You can do something about it, or you can move on out a' here," he responded.

Ruth put out her cigarette in her sink faucet. "That's what we thinking about doing," she said and did not elaborate. "Let's go."

The boy sat in front of the television set, head cupped in his hands. The words and attitudes floated over his body with no impact whatsoever on his young mind. At his age, he was still spared from the ugly history of his country and his own uncertain future. Race issues, in particular, meant nothing to him as of yet. There were no races in the cartoon worlds he presently observed.

Listening to his daughter speak, however, Grady thought again about the reward money in the Chen murder. The idea approached his consciousness like some gremlin from the recesses of his mind. Could money be a balm for all of their current situations? Could not one hundred thousand dollars go a long way for everyone?

To those ends, he could not help himself from asking before they walked out the door: "If you could leave San Francisco, where would you go?"

His daughter gave him a curious look. "I don't know," she said hesitantly and suspiciously. To her, it had been a strange and surprising question. "I guess Oakland," she said. "I could not take it there a few years ago, but I have a different attitude and outlook now. That's where all the other black people in the Bay Area live, anyway. I know some people over there now, too. The white people don't want you anywhere else. But then there's Vallejo and Fairfield. I don't know anyone there. Why you askin'? You got some dollars hidden under the mattress?"

"If I had some, you know I would help ya'll out. But don't give up hope," the father said, careful not to specify right now.

The boy continued to be hypnotized by the television screen, even as they were leaving.

CHAPTER XI

After returning from seeing his daughter, Grady remembered to ask McTeague to fix the hallway light. He had caught McTeague outside the building and McTeague lumbered up the stairs, fiddled with some wires, and left with the hallway bulb shining brighter than ever. McTeague then lumbered back down the stairs, huffing and puffing and sweating profusely. It was a physical affect that seemed disproportionate to the work he had done. While McTeague worked on the light, Grady noticed a tattoo on the big man's arm that said "Fugitive," and Grady could not figure out what it meant.

For now though, Grady was content because the hallway light was now strong and bright and the bulb itself seemed to symbolize a new hope for him, and perhaps for his family as well. He had thought more about cashing in on the $100,000 reward on the bus ride back from seeing his daughter and grandson, and the money would not be so much for him, but for them. After having been inspired by the serenity of the postcard image of the bay during their family walk along the waters – the boy had joined them for this excursion, while Grady was not sure of Chuck's whereabouts later in the day -- Grady now saw the reward money -- indeed his very witnessing of the crime -- as having been ordained by God himself: a God who Grady would find new interest in subsequently.

For two weeks, while the reward held at $100,000, the police developed no new leads, and the media reduced the Chen murder to a back-story because of the lack of new information. Grady pondered his next move, while a number of events peppered his daily experience.

One of them involved an interaction with a worker at his building who invited him to a church service. Evangeline Bishop, who worked for an accounting firm on his building's 17th floor, had hit him up again recently, and based on all the things that were going on in his life, he decided he would go this time.

In the past, he had rejected her offers, for various reasons. But in light of recent events, perhaps the sermon might provide some kind of clarity to his current dilemma and shed light on a world that was becoming ever more uncontrollable and confusing.

Wizard had once said people were all living in an age of hate and fear, brought on by materialism. "The manifestations of this hate and fear are depravity, greed, and desperation," Wizard had said, and Grady had believed and understood what he had said on a basic level.

Basically what he had said was that something had changed in the world and that something was wrong with it now. The world was headed in the wrong direction. Grady had believed his words and thought maybe a church visit might be in order about now, more than ever. Grady still believed in God on a fundamental level. Maybe God would give him some advice regarding the Chen murder also.

Grady had not been to church since his wife's funeral 15 years ago. There were not many churches in San Francisco that he could relate to, and there were hardly any Baptist ones. Those were the kinds he once attended growing up in the South. Many of the Baptist ones that still existed were over in Bayview-Hunter's Point, near his daughter's area, and he didn't want to catch the bus over there on a regular basis.

Grady was aware that a substantial portion of San Francisco's remaining black citizens, particularly the older ones, still attended regularly. Some even journeyed over to Oakland and the East Bay to go to church on Sunday. Therefore, he was not surprised at Evangeline's faith or her zeal, but he still said "no" when previously asked to attend church with her. He always came up with different excuses, depending on the situation.

Unlike most of the building tenants he knew, Evangeline Bishop seemed centered and never in a hurry. She always exerted a calming influence on him. In general, she was a "solid" woman to Grady. She was the kind that *used* to exist, way back in the past. The fact that she could still remain in a rapidly changing city like San Francisco was a testament to her patience and grace.

A little older than Grady, Evangeline was not beautiful, but she was not unattractive either. She dressed conservatively, not flashy, as the overwhelming majority of people Grady came in contact with did. She was darker in complexion than Grady. Evangeline's hair was salt and pepper gray, thick and wavy, conveying, unintentionally, a kind of dignity, wisdom, and even regality. She was short in stature and she still had all her teeth, which were white and pearly. When she spoke, there was that same touch of the mid-20th century southern United States in her voice, similar to Grady's own.

She had, in fact, been born and raised in Louisiana before she joined her husband, who came West with many other post-World War II blacks looking for work. Her husband eventually found work as a house painter and carpenter, Grady had learned from Evangeline over the years. Secretarial work would become Evangeline's specialty.

The accounting company she worked for as a bookkeeper and office manager used to be located in the Sunset District on Irving Street, but had expanded in recent years and had secured a key location in the office building where it was now.

She had considered not making the move downtown with its hectic atmosphere, but she still felt strong at her age and her company still wanted to keep her. She expected to retire in a year or two with a full pension. Grady had always secretly envied her. There was an invulnerability about her.

He had asked her once how a nice person like her could work in a sometimes unstable place like downtown San Francisco. She had replied that continuing to work was still "God's will" for her life. Grady did not feel like arguing with that, as he was not sure what God thought of his own life.

Though he knew he needed some kind of guidance in his life in general, he was not prepared to relate his problems to anyone at the church directly. He was only looking for something to speak to him one way or another through some kind of religious experience. Since God was apparently "favoring" him with the reward money at this point, Grady thought that it wouldn't hurt to have God see him trying to do his part. Going to church couldn't hurt. However, the more fundamental Christian beliefs he had had as a child had been replaced by a kind of superstitious cynicism over the years.

Grady was happy that he had worn the right outfit on Sunday morning, because Evangeline and her husband were finely dressed. Evangeline wore a large, navy blue hat, with a wide brim and a stitching of flowers on one side. Her husband was equally dapper, driving his large sedan with great ease and skill, not at all intimidated by San Francisco's ruggedly hilly and sometimes speedy downtown streets. Grady envied the general simplicity of the husband's approach to life.

"I used ta wuhk down heah yeahs ago, didn't I honey?" he said, through a polished baritone voice.

"Henry was a painter and carpenter," Evangeline reminded Grady, with a combination of pride and admiration in her voice. "Some of these buildings he helped build. Maybe even where you live."

"Oh, ah really don't remembuh which ones," Henry said humbly, as he calmly and smoothly negotiated a turn with his big car.

Grady liked Henry because he had a grace, personal dignity, warmth, and self-confidence that were appealing. He reminded Grady of some of the old black gentlemen back in the South, in days past. What had happened to those days, he thought to himself, while sitting in the car's backseat, and watching San Francisco life go by out the window. Henry had been preserved well over the years it seemed. What was his secret, Grady thought?

Soon they were turning from Franklin Street onto Geary Boulevard, heading toward the avenues. Grady had not been past Van Ness Avenue in a couple years. He never had any reason. He used to go to the Fillmore District years ago to hear jazz bands, but many of those clubs were now gone, along with San Francisco's vanishing black people.

Of all the faces he saw now, the majority, were white, Asian, or Hispanic, and the black people he did see were not worth much. They walked around bitter and angry, hard-looking, unkempt, destitute, and were on occasion, mentally ill. Grady thought again that you would be hard-pressed to find a professional-looking black man or woman in San Francisco these days, when just 15 years ago or so that was not the case. Where were the black people in suits now?

There had never been a multitude of blacks in San Francisco at any given time, but the current population was still drying up at a fast rate. One might be better off going over the Oakland, as his daughter had said. It was like some form of racial extermination, but Grady could not really put his finger on the causes and effects of the situation. Still, he was impressed with his present company, who were like a breath of fresh air.

"Ya'll still live in the city," Grady ventured from the back seat, as the car pulled up to a stop light at Divisadero and Sutter.

"Yes, we still live in the city," Evangeline said, followed by a quiet sigh that Grady noticed. "But we're thinking about leaving and moving to Fairfield. San Francisco is getting too expensive and too wild and crazy. The Lord brought us here years ago, but the Lord also tells you when it's time to leave a place. Don't you agree?"

Grady was a little surprised that she seemed to be directing this question to him, as if he had some insight on the plans of God.

"I cannot not really say, Miss Evangeline," he said humbly. "Me and the Lord ain't been talking in a while. Not since my wife died in 81'.

Both she and her husband smiled at the apparent quaintness of what Grady had said about his relationship to God.

"Well hopefully you can fix that this morning," Evangeline said, and turned around from the front seat to smile at him. "I think you will like our pastor," she added.

"I hope so," Grady said, the only way he felt qualified to respond at the moment.

The old man said nothing that time, only continuing to drive smoothly, until they pulled up next to a white building on Broderick Street.

This was the church. It was a small, old, and unassuming white building that seemed to literally sprout out from the ground. Grady had perhaps passed it before some years ago when he wandered through this area of town, but probably paid little attention to it. To him, it would have been just another black church. He wasn't attending back then either.

When Grady got inside, he had to admit that he felt a peace come over him that he could not describe. The people were friendly, all black faces, mostly older people around the age of Evangeline and her husband. There were some school-age children, but few teenagers.

After he had been inside for about 10 minutes, a woman started playing an organ and this soothed him even more. There was something about returning to the cradle of his own unique heritage that made him feel comfortable.

"I ain't been to church in years," he whispered to
Evangeline Bishop's husband. "I feel kinda guilty about it."

Bishop laughed. "I know a hunnert guys like you. You ain't
no different.' Jes relax. Pastor's pretty good. Been aroun' a long
time."

When the pastor eventually came in, he shook hands with
various people as he made his way through the aisle. He wore a
black robe that made him look spiritual, setting him apart from
the congregation. He looked to be about 10 years younger than
Grady, but despite his age, he possessed an enormous vitality
and energy that was evident in just about every movement he
made. It was evident in his steps, to his facial expressions, to
his handshake.

"How you doin' brother" he said heartily to Grady. "Nice
to see you today!"

"He works in my building downtown," Evangeline
explained.

"Been trying to get him here for a while."

Grady smiled, and so did the pastor.

"Well, glad to have you here brother."

"Thank you, pastor," Grady said, and shook the man's hand.
He had a solid and seemingly sincere grip.

Grady then watched as the energetic preacher skipped up
the few stairs leading to the altar, while the organ continued to
play. He laid down the big, black Bible he had been carrying
on the dais in front of him and looked down into it, perhaps
going over one last time what he was about to say. The church,
meanwhile, as small as it was, was not crowded. It was as if this
man, Reverend Mapple, was their own private pastor.

Grady wanted to feel privileged over this arrangement; but
he could not, because he was still not completely relaxed overall.

He had not been to church in so long, that he did not know what he should be thinking. Therefore, he decided to ignore the spiritual import of the experience and treat it as if a show were about to take place. This perspective allowed him to relax more and not feel compelled to express himself individually. He would be a non-invested spectator until the service came to a conclusion. What was wrong with such an approach? After all, he was only a visitor on this day anyway.

Other than Grady and his two companions, there were two other families, about six single people, and a few little children. By the time the sermon began, the young children were sent downstairs for their own study, depleting the ranks in the sanctuary even further.

Though a spirit within him told him that he should run out and leave the building, Grady began to feel more content after a while. He did not know exactly what was going to happen from one moment to the next in this particular church, but he began to feel patient enough to wait it out. He read in his program that the subject for the sermon that morning was going to be "Maintaining Integrity in the Modern World." Grady was not sure exactly what the word "integrity" would mean in the context of a church sermon, but he knew that "integrity" was something good, something that people should have in life.

"Are there any first-time visitors with us today?" the preacher asked of the congregation after the organ's music had stopped. He already knew that Grady was a visitor, as he had been introduced, but it was the routine to ask of the congregation at-large anyway.

Grady stood up slowly, but with confidence. All eyes of the church were on him. He introduced himself, related some personal information, was greeted warmly by the pastor and members, and was invited to return anytime he liked.

The organist then started to play again, while the pastor took his seat behind his pulpit. During this time, a few more people trickled in, looked around, uttered a few hushed "hellos" to some others, and took their seats. Then, a man sitting near the front took to the altar and instructed the congregation to stand to its feet for the singing of the first hymn of the morning. It was one that Grady had sung before, but not in many years. The singing of it almost brought tears to his eyes. He tried to hold them back so as not to appear weak and foolish.

"Blessed Assurance
Jesus is Mine
Oh what a foretaste Of Glory Divine.
Heir of salvation
Purchase of God,
Born of His Spirit,
Washed in His blood.
This is my story, this is my song,
Praising my Savior all the day long;
This is my story, this is my song,
Praising my Savior all the day long...."

Grady had not wanted the song to end. He could have sung it all morning, and though he felt self-conscious about singing too loudly, his voice could easily be heard by those around him. The words of the song, the unity and harmony of the voices around him, and the positive memories the song engendered within him, filled him with simultaneous comfort, joy, and hope. He began to feel very happy he had come, and happier than he had been in a while.

A few more people trickled in during the song, to the point where the place became three quarters full. After the congregation took its seats again, the church announcements were read. Grady took this time to look through the church bulletin once again. Overall, it was slight, with just the bare facts about church business, a kind of reflection of the relatively small congregation assembled.

He wondered whether black churches might be on their way out of popularity altogether, at least in San Francisco. After all, he did not know anyone else in the part of San Francisco where he lived who went to church regularly. He felt the urge to ask the Bishops this question and he resolved to ask them later during the car ride home.

After the announcements, several more songs were sung, to which Grady added an even louder voice than he had on the first one. He even drew Evangeline's attention, though she did not look directly at him while he sang. During the singing this time, a half dozen more people entered the church, giving it the fuller look that Grady believed a church should have. He found himself looking around, seeing who was who.

The offering was taken up by two young men, one of whom had led in the singing. Grady put in ten dollars. He suddenly felt generous.

Next came the morning prayer, delivered by Reverend Mapple. "Dear Father in Heaven, we come to you united together in your house to give you praise and worship on another Sunday morning. Today, we leave our worldly cares and concerns outside so that we can fellowship with clean hearts and clean minds. We know that we are not perfect, oh Lord.

All of us come here with something on our minds, something in our hearts that we are battling and dealing with daily. And we seek your eternal guidance and direction because we cannot do it without you. We cannot do it alone. We should not even try to go it alone in this world.

"We thank you for this house of worship, for this place to come to fellowship—this ship in the storm, to which you have appointed me captain. You have put me here to shepherd these people and lead them. And as your humble servant, I pray that you give me the wisdom to say the right words and inspire the right emotions to produce the right behavior in the members of this flock. If there is any malice in me, remove it; if there is any fear in me, remove it; if there is any doubt in me, remove that also. Because all of these have no place with true faith.

"Shape my words as they come out of my mouth and fashion the ears and hearts that receive them. It is in all of these things that we pray in your son Jesus' name, Amen."

The prayer had the effect of calming Grady even more, like a sedative. He felt that he had been initiated into something, or that a protective covering had been placed on all of them. At the moment, he had no anxiety and did not even think of the outside world. The only world that existed was the world of his most immediate environment.

Grady believed the pastor to be sincere. One could hear it in his voice and could see it in his demeanor, as after the prayer, he again took his seat behind the dais.

He was replaced there by a young girl from the congregation. She also opened up a bible she had carried there with her. "Please open your bibles," said the girl, who could not have been more than 15, "to the Gospel According to Luke. I will be reading from the King James Version, Chapter 10, verses 25-37."

The girl waited while the now healthy congregation gathered itself, rose to its feet, reached for Bibles from the pews, shared others, and flipped pages. Grady shared a Bible with Evangeline, though he paid only partial attention to the actual text. He sort of only looked at the book as a whole. By the time the young girl was about to read, he had forgotten what exact scripture they were supposed to be reading.

He did not own a Bible of his own. His wife had had one but he had not seen it since they moved from the old house in the Sunset District.

The young girl began to read:

> *And, behold, a certain lawyer stood up, and tempted him, saying, Master, what shall I do to inherit eternal life?*
> *He said unto him, What is written in the law?*
> *How readest thou?*
> *And he answering said, Thou shalt love the Lord thy God with all thy heart, and with all thy soul, and with all thy strength, and with all thy mind; and thy neighbour as thyself.*
> *And he said unto him, Thou hast answered right: this do, and thou shalt live.*
> *But he, willing to justify himself, said unto Jesus, And who is my neighbour?*
> *And Jesus answering said, A certain man went down from Jerusalem to Jericho, and fell among thieves, which stripped him of his raiment, and wounded him, and departed, leaving him half dead.*
> *And by chance there came down a certain priest that way: and when he saw him, he passed by on the other side.*
> *And likewise a Levite, when he was at the place, came and looked on him, and passed by on the other side.*

But a certain Samaritan, as he journeyed, came where he was: and when he saw him, he had compassion on him,

And went to him, and bound up his wounds, pouring in oil and wine, and set him on his own beast, and brought him to an inn, and took care of him.

And on the morrow when he departed, he took out two pence, and gave them to the host, and said unto him, Take care of him; and whatsoever thou spendest more, when I come again, I will repay thee.

Which now of these three, thinkest thou, was neighbour unto him that fell among the thieves?" And he said, He that shewed mercy on him. Then said Jesus unto him, Go, and do thou likewise.

The young girl quietly closed the book after the reading, retaking her seat in the pews.

Reverend Mapple quickly took his place at the podium.

"What in the world is going on in this country?" he asked through tightly controlled firmness and passion. "I have asked the question before. I need to ask it again. What in the world is happening to this country?" He was more demonstrative the second time, getting Grady's attention even more.

Grady had not paid great attention to the reading, recognizing only the word "Samaritan," acknowledging somewhere in his mind that the word had something to do with being a good person. He looked around at the others in the church. They were paying strict attention to their pastor's words and Grady began to make a conscious effort to do the same.

The pastor continued. "I ask the question to put it into your mind again, so that when you leave here, you might ask it of yourselves this week and in the weeks to follow. Because the problem is that we forget.

"In life, we hear about doing the right thing. It is said to us and repeated to us, but then when we get out there in the real world and are confronted by stress and strain, our basic beliefs... they drain away like water.

"I'm not saying that we are always afraid to do the right thing. I'm saying that sometimes out there, we simply forget what it is we really believe. So, I am here to reinforce some of the things I have spoken to you about in the past."

Reverend Mapple took a brief moment to gather himself.

"I'm calling this sermon, 'Maintaining Your Integrity in the Modern World,'" he continued. "The first question then would be, 'what is 'integrity'? There is a definition in the dictionary for this word certainly; but it has other meanings, like many words do. But, for my purposes—and this is a church after all—I would like to concentrate on the definition that has to do with having high moral values.

"Now the dictionary does not specify a particular religion where integrity is concerned. The word could refer to any faith. But the word is a part of the English language and a part of America and I will use it to apply specifically in this case to the Christian faith.

"On hearing the word 'integrity,' I know you all already know what it means. You've have heard it before. It is a challenging word, that's for sure. It is a 'high-road' word like 'moral' and 'ethical,' in a culture like today that chooses more often to take the 'lowest roads' when it comes to behavior and doing what is right by God. Am I right about that?"

"Amen," the congregation, including Evangeline and Henry, responded uniformly and enthusiastically to the pastor. Grady said nothing because the pastor's question had overtaken him too quickly. He would be ready for it the next time.

"But the word 'integrity' is still there and still has a bearing on how we live in today's world, at least for now," the pastor continued.

"Right now in this world, we have to worry about this word—integrity—before it is removed from our dictionaries altogether, and is no longer seen as important at all anymore. Then we will really have a problem. For now though, the word still has *some* meaning to our daily lives, at home, at work, in the streets, while driving in our cars, and within our government.

"I would like to define the word for you here, as doing what is proper and best by an absolute set of standards, whether someone is around watching you do it or not. You see, one does not necessarily have to believe in God to have integrity. The word itself is how we say -- neutral. But we as Christians choose to use the best aspects of the word and apply its key principles to our own faith where our absolute standards of living daily life are used in service to God and his principles. Do you see where I am headed, church?"

"Amen," the congregation agreed again, louder this time, and Grady again kept his "amen" to himself. The spirit of being a mere bystander in the church had again settled over him.

"We need to show Christian integrity, at all times!" the pastor charged to the congregation, this time slamming his fist briskly on the pulpit, in a fit of what could only be called, *righteous* anger. "Just like the Samaritan! That man was not a friend of the man he helped, but a stranger, who obliged to help another out of the goodness of his heart.

"Just like the Samaritan. That man was not a friend of the man he helped, but a stranger, who obliged to help another out of the goodness of his heart. Now, most of us, surely most of you older members, have heard this story ever since you were children sitting like the little ones downstairs right now. This is just my point: times may change, but the message stays the same. Human beings might change, but God stays the same. He vows never to change. And we cannot change our basic beliefs either. Like the Samaritan, we must always be ready to show the integrity of our faith to the world and what better way than by extending hands of charity, goodness, and love to the less fortunate. This might sound like a tall order, but it can be done, especially with God's power, as given through his Holy Spirit."

"Amen!" came several more affirmations from the congregation. Grady meekly gave an "amen" this time, mostly not to appear out of step with the others. He found himself mostly observing the preacher's performance—the job he was doing— more so than listening to what the man had to say.

"Remember folks," Reverend Mapple re-emphasized, "the Helper, God's Holy Spirit, is always there to help us to 'do the right thing,' if we, in fact, are willing, to do those right things. It begins and ends with our wills, does it not?

"I'm not gonna be here too long for you this morning. But I want you to understand my point, the points that I am trying to make. I am saying that you must take on new attitudes of service out there in this world. Most importantly, you must see your fellow humans differently. Do not see them as objects, obstacles, or things to be used and abused, but as people to be helped and loved, especially in their times of need. I know this can be hard, especially when some people can be cold hearted and ungrateful. But that does not concern you. For we are soldiers, soldiers of God's love. Love is what we are all about here. Love is the highest gift of the spirit and it can do incredible things. Am I right church!"

"Yes Lord! Thank you Jesus!" came several stronger affirmations from the congregation.

"That Samaritan was not a friend of the Jews, but an enemy. His situation was also about race and the Bible wants us to understand that. Jesus wanted us to understand that. That is why he told the story. We assume that the man leaving Jerusalem for Jericho was a Jewish person. And we know from Bible history and from the Bible itself that Jews and Samaritans of that time did not get along together. We as black people know more than any other people in the world about the race problem. Don't we? Yet, in the Bible story, we have a situation where charity is specifically given and fear is overcome, despite someone's race or background. Am I right about that, church?"

"Yes Lord!" a woman near the back, on the other side of the aisle, heartily agreed in response.

"The man's own people did not help him," the pastor continued, "a priest and a Levite. But the Samaritan did. Imagine how much that man had to overcome to do "the right thing": prejudice, social backlash and revenge, financial sacrifice, and sacrifice of his time and physical effort. Yet there are some of you here right now who might not even give a quarter to a bum down on Market Street if you saw the person in need. You might step right over him. I tell you, we must change our ways church, or we are all doomed to the fate of the rest of the world!"

"You right pastor, you right about it!" a man across the aisle from Grady said.

The last series of exchanges left Grady newly riveted to the pastor and the whole scene. The pastor spoke with a power and passion that Grady had not seen in a long time. For a brief moment, Grady even found himself frightened, but could not explain why.

"What did the Samaritan have, church?" the pastor asked teasingly, but seriously, of his flock. "What's the word for today?"

"Integrity!" several people shouted from different places in the pews.

"That's right!" the pastor affirmed. "It is good to know that you are paying attention to your pastor this morning. But will you be remembering an hour from now, when you are on the freeway and somebody cuts you off in traffic? Or when someone looks at you 'the wrong way' out in the street? When someone needs a favor and you feel you are too busy or too tired? When a co-worker gets you mad over something meaningless? When you are called upon in some situation to go the extra mile? What does integrity mean to you and will you remember it and apply it in your life every day?

"With that in mind, and before closing, I will give you four reasons why people, even Christian people, often forget, or altogether dismiss, what feels right by their consciences; and I expect you to write these down so you will be able to remember them when you see them coming in your lives."

There was a pen sticking out from a pen holder at the back of the pew, but Grady did not pick it up to use it. He still considered himself mostly a spectator during the service, and he did not want to write down any promises he might not be able to keep.

"Number one," the preacher said. "The first reason why many of us resist showing the integrity that the Samaritan showed is because many of us are selfish and self-centered. We don't want to give away anything where we don't get anything in return. This is a 'buy and sell society'—commerce and capitalism—and that gets into everything now, even simple favors. 'Why should

I help you out, if I am not getting something out of it?' But, as we know, that is not the Christian way.

"The Christian way is to be 'self-less' at all times, to die to the self, as Jesus put it, in favor of service to God and His standards. Those standards involve helping other people. Our mission, church, to put it simply, is to reach out for the sake of reaching out. Out of love, and the goodness of our hearts, because we love and care for our fellow men and women, because we love and care for our God."

There were more "amens" heard around the church, including from Evangeline, who sat right next to Grady.

"Number two," the pastor continued, and the pastor's words continued to overwhelm Grady, like a deluge he had not expected. "Many of us do not reach out to others because we are afraid to do it. We are afraid of the responsibilities attached to our charity, we are afraid of interacting with other people, we are afraid to open our hearts in a closed-hearted world. We are afraid that if we open our own hearts that it will sting even more when we are burned by somebody the next time.

"But what if we are burned by someone in life? So what? It does not have to hurt. God is there. He's got our backs. We can take it. He is our measuring stick, not this world. Let that person think that they have gotten the best of you. What do you care? We do not live by the standards of the world anyway. Am I right?"

"Yes, Pastor!" someone said.

"I'm not saying to let people have their way with you, to walk all over you. I'm saying that you should not let the world and its ways dictate how you should live and prevent you from doing what you know is right by God's standards. Your reward is in Heaven, not on this earth, and you should never, ever be afraid of what people can do to you. Because even in death, are not we the winners, through Christ our Lord. Am I right about that too, church?"

"Amen!" came the loudest agreement yet from the assembly. Grady continued to listen with everyone else, and he felt he was being inspired internally in some way, but he remained mute.

"So we should not be afraid to reach out to others," the pastor said, concluding his second point. "Because God has not given his people the spirit of fear, but of power and of love and a sound mind."

"Amen Pastor!" someone near the front offered again in response.

"Third," the pastor enjoined again, "we are often Un-Samaritan simply because we are forgetful. We forget who we are as Christians. We get too caught up in the moment and want to obey our bodies first and not our spirits. It is a fast-paced, selfish world where even we Christians are sometimes caught off our guard and find ourselves making decisions out of speed and not out of integrity.

"I encourage you, therefore, to always stop and think before you act. Think about who you are and what it is you believe. If you must, think about me and what I said. Think about your church and your church members, but mostly, think about your God, who is watching your behavior, because he is. And learn to slow down. The Holy Spirit will help you to do that too."

"And lastly," the preacher said, "with regard to our fast-moving world, I cannot state it any clearer that we need to slow down and think. We cannot allow the world to force us to move at its pace. Because, as we know, this world is impatient, and we as Christians must show the world what patience is.

"Trust me church, patience itself can be a pathway to integrity and the idea of patience is lost in the modern world. Don't you think the Samaritan had patience in what he did, stopping the progress of his own life, to come to the aid of the life of someone else? His was a high form of integrity, and it was through patience also." "Remember then," the pastor then added, as he was about to close, "these four factors in your daily lives, and I will, of course, be reminding you of them from time to time. Remember the Good Samaritan, not as just a nice tale about a nice man in the bible. But it is real-world story, more real than ever. It has specific meaning in our lives and to the very health of this country. The Samaritan's actions were based in integrity, Christian integrity. Integrity can be lost, and we are losing it today out in the non-Christian world for sure. Lost families and a lost country. This is where we are today. But this is not your calling, because this is not what we are about as Christians. We are about love. That's what we are about here! Am I right about it, church?"

"Amen!" came some final strong affirmations from the general congregation.

"Do the right thing, church, and God will do right by you. Now stand to your feet while the organist plays."

The organist assumed her position at her instrument and soon the church was filled with sweet sounds again, and Grady sensed that the service would soon come to an end. The pastor had overwhelmed him with words and ideas and Grady tried to recapture his bearings as the pastor sat down behind the pulpit. Then a woman, accompanied by the organist, sang a solo.

The music was soothing to Grady and he did not want to leave for the sake of the music alone. He wanted to be confined to the peace of the church. He had not experienced such feelings since he was a child, although then he could not interpret them. As an adult, he now understood the value of a kind of mental and spiritual serenity.

However, though he had been impressed by the sermon, little of its essential message sunk into him. For one thing, he could not understand all of it, being only a one-time visitor. He did not have the institutional knowledge that the rest of the congregation had accumulated over the years. Some aspects of the bible story he could recall; others he could not. After the sermon, he still considered himself a visitor, someone that was passing through, who might or might not return.

"That was nice," he whispered to Evangeline Bishop at the end of the solo.

"I am glad you liked it," Evangeline whispered back softly. "Maybe we can get you back here again."

Maybe Miss Evangeline," he said, still feeling the need to whisper. "I'll have to think about it."

As the organist played following the musical solo, the pastor returned to the pulpit where he asked if there was anyone in attendance who wanted to give their lives to Jesus Christ, receive eternal life in Heaven based on that act, and become members of the church.

Grady sat in his seat and looked down again at his program. Instinctively, he knew that this sort of call was routine in Baptist services. He also knew that there were specifics involved in it, like getting up and going forward, and that would mean more time spent in the church. He was not prepared to do that today, so he remained in his seat until the call was over and it was time to go. During that time, a silence permeated the sanctuary. A woman near the front got up and accepted the pastor's call to accept Jesus Christ as her personal savior. There was some mild applause over her decision.

"Is there anyone else?" the pastor said, extending his hand toward those seated, like a shepherd trying to bring in lost members of a flock. He looked briefly down at Grady, who did not move one way or the other, in either mind or body. He intentionally averted the pastor's gaze and inside was anticipating the conclusion of the proceedings. The warmth he had felt during the service was cooling off gradually.

For her part, Evangeline Bishop was torn over how to approach her co-worker in this very solemn moment, resolving after a few moments that she would have to be patient and talk to Grady a little more about his beliefs before trying to encourage him to commit his life to the service of God and the church. An impulse that she interpreted as coming from God inspired her to hold back for the moment.

The woman came forward and was formally introduced to the church as a new person seeking membership in both the church and in "the kingdom of God," after which she was led away for a new member's orientation. Then the organist played, and the pastor instructed the congregation, which now filled some ninety percent of the church, to rise to its feet for the benediction. The pastor closed his eyes, as did everyone else, including Grady, who held hands with those at either side of him.

"Now may the Lord keep you and bless you this week and forever. May he enter your hearts and show you his will, purpose, and direction. May you always be open to receive his guidance. Go from here, members of Christ's body, seeking integrity in a fallen world. Seeking to be like the Samaritan, who did not seek rewards for himself, but the rewards of serving his fellow man. Go in blessings and peace. Amen."

"Amen," came a solemn and subdued response from the congregation this time, and even Grady mumbled the word. Upon doing so, the peace he felt that day was complete in him. Even though the effects of the sermon had waned somewhat, he felt that he had accomplished something by sitting through an entire church service for the first time in a long time. He "felt" somewhat "holy," just by achieving that accomplishment alone.

⟋𝓎⟍

"Thanks for bringing me along today," he said again to Evangeline and her husband as they walked to the car. "The pastor was good and he made me feel good. We all need that once in a while."

"You welcome, of course," Henry Bishop said easily and heartily. "You kin come necks week if ya like. All ya have to do is ask," he added and shook Grady's hand.

But Grady rapidly thought for a moment about how much he liked his Sundays off and politely declined. Sunday was the day that he slept in the most, like a lot of San Franciscans did.

They all got into the car.

"You know the church could use more matured men like yourself," Evangeline said to Grady without trying to sound too pushy, once they were inside the car, and headed back to Grady's apartment.

"That might be nice one day soon, but let me think about it," Grady said cordially. "I need to know where I am with God before I start making any commitments."

"I understand," Evangeline said. "But God does not expect you to change for him. You can just come to him as you are right now. And he will work with you to make you who he wants you to be."

"I understand dear," Grady said through a somewhat patronizing tone that he could not control for some reason. "But I got to be where I want to be right now. You know what I'm saying?"

Both the Bishops understood what he meant and did not press him on it. "Well, we are always here for you and so is the Lord, of course," Evangeline added.

"I know he is," Grady again responded cordially. "Even though I might not act like it sometimes."

This initiated a laugh among the three of them over the vagaries of human nature.

They dropped him off at his apartment about 20 minutes later.

⌒m⌒

Though he had not made the somewhat obvious connection between the sermon and the present circumstances in his life, Grady was, however, at least able to acknowledge that what had come over him during the service had somehow managed to follow him home. It colored what he saw and experienced once he returned to downtown.

Somehow the people in the street looked nicer and less angry, the streets themselves looked less dirty, and were less offensive to his senses. Everyone now seemed to be just part and parcel of a struggling humanity, which would always come up short in its relation to an all-powerful God.

He could not articulate the feelings he was having, but he carried these feelings with him after the service ended, like he had been to a mountaintop and experienced a peace and an understanding that the world in general was sorely lacking.

Once inside his building, there was quiet. McTeague was not in his office and there was no noise coming from Spike's apartment, certainly nothing like the other day. The new light bulb illuminated Grady's hallway perfectly. He was also willing to dismiss his suspicions that something was going on between Lorraine and the Hispanic father. Presently, he had no desire to judge.

Despite the superficial good feelings resulting from an apparent post-church after glow, it did not take long for him to assume the ornery disposition that had invaded his personality within the past six months or so. His mood began to change late in the evening, just after nightfall, with the arrival of a spring moon that hovered over the city like a bad sign of something. It was unaccompanied by any breeze. Instead there was a humid stillness in the night, which was very unusual for city weather.

Grady had his window open and, looking up at the sky from it, his existence hit him in the face. He realized that he was alone and that he was lonely. There was a whole world out there, but it was not his world. It was not the kind of world that he wanted, not the kind with which he could talk to or relate, and it resembled nothing like the world of his past. These realizations made him mildly depressed and a little embittered. The church influence had worn off in the face of urban reality. Or maybe the church experience had merely shed light on what he was lacking overall. Whatever it was, he felt an existential emptiness looking out the window at that moment. Grady craved the uplift which the movement of the cool San

Francisco air might have given him, but it was as if the city was determined to balance out any of the spiritual gains he had made, because the air remained warm and still.

Caving into himself, he thought, "This world is against me and I got to get somethin' back." He turned on the television to see if there was any more news on the Edward Chen case. There was not, but he knew that it had not been solved, for if it had, there would have been a big celebration of the fact.

After some pondering into the late evening, he decided that he would *finally report what he had seen.* "It's time for me to get somethin' for me and my family," he said to himself. "I'm not gonna live forever and this world ain't gonna give me nothin'."

When he made the pronouncement to himself, he had a bottle in his hand. He drank as the night wore on and as the stale moon rose higher in the sky.

The next day at work, as he contemplated how he would approach the phone call to the police, he was greeted by a visitor at his guard desk around about 11 am.

"Scuse me mate," a tall white man with auburn hair, eyebrows, and mustache, said to him. "Could ya direct me to East Gate Financial Services?" The man smiled jovially after he had asked the question.

Grady was alone at the desk at the moment. Buddy had been fired recently for abandoning his post, leaving early without permission, and several other violations. Tony was now working Buddy's old shift, but he was away checking on something. Grady looked up at the man who spoke and responded professionally, as he always did.

After the man had left, Grady's heartbeat began to accelerate; while at the same time, the lobby appeared to move in slow motion. He felt that there was something unusual about the man he had just helped, but he could not put his finger on it. Maybe it was the man's accent that had unsettled him.

It took a moment for it to register, but after gathering himself and reviewing the things he had committed to memory, Grady believed that he had just seen the man who had murdered Edward Chen and had just directed the man to the 9th floor.

CHAPTER XII

After the shock had worn off from what Grady *thought* he had seen, he quickly realized that before jumping to any conclusions, he would have to see the man again to be sure.

He did not believe that more than one person in San Francisco could have eyebrows like that. They were a burnt red or auburn and they were thick. They also matched the color of his moustache while being a shade darker than his wavy hair. His height looked the same as well. To top it all off, Grady was sure that the man was wearing the same long, dark overcoat he had worn the night of the attack. Aside from these visual facts and cues, Grady was not sure exactly where to go from here, outside of waiting for the man to come back downstairs. He might be able to create a reason to go upstairs when Tony came back to the desk, but he was not one who was good at creating diversions. He was not even all that good at lying, and, at the moment, he could think of no reason at all to have to go up to the 9th floor. Whatever he did, he would have to wait for Tony to return anyway.

What accent was that? He thought to himself. *What country?* He had heard it before somewhere.

There were all kinds of accents in San Francisco. It could be one of a number. Unfortunately for him, Grady had not gotten the man's name. Then he would have more specific evidence to deliver to the police when he called them. How could this happen? He was on the verge of reporting the crime, and the man he thought he had seen commit the murder suddenly turns up in his building, right in front of his face. What did this mean?

He had been to church for the first time in over a dozen years, just over 24 hours ago. Since that experience, Grady had begun to believe that now was probably the time to spill what he knew. It had been almost a full month, from that night, and now this man had delivered himself to Grady on a silver platter. Surely there was something beyond him at work here. Maybe God was trying to tell him that it definitely was time to divulge the truth that only he knew.

Grady, meanwhile, was shocked that the man had the nerve to continue to walk around the downtown area. White people, he thought, were capable of a lot of things, but this was too much. From what he had just seen, the man looked well-to-do and probably educated. He must know what had been going on in the news for the past month. Grady's mind now moved at speeds of thought it had not reached in years. If his body were to be asked to keep up with the pace of his mind right now, it would be impossible and he might collapse.

And what was the man doing in Grady's own building? He needed a reason to visit the 9th floor. He ran through some of Buddy's old tricks for leaving the desk behind and by the time Tony finally returned, Grady had a large manila envelope in his hand with the words 'East Gate Financial' written on the front. Before Tony could sit down, Grady jumped up, saying over his shoulder that a visitor had dropped off the envelope, which needed to be delivered urgently to East Gate Services.

Tony bought the story and Grady immediately headed towards the elevator banks.

He might have felt guilty about making up such an excuse another time, but this time Grady convinced himself that he was doing God's work, because he could come up with no other explanation for the convergence of recent events.

The 9th floor was one of those floors with a single large client: East Gate Financial Services. It only had one entrance. From the elevator exit, Grady could only get a view of the secretary and her desk through the firm's glass doors. Waving kindly at her, as if he were doing a security check, he returned to the lobby after seeing no other figures in the office other than her. He had no firm reason to enter the office and search for anyone, regardless of his suspicions.

By the time he got off from work, two hours later, Grady did not see the mysterious man come through the lobby again, and he had been at his post most of that time. Therefore, on this day, Grady was unable to verify the man's identity, leaving him puzzled.

"Maybe it wasn't him," he pondered, before catching himself. "Then again, maybe it was." Despite his uncertainty, he did not want to wait around the building to get another look. He did not know how long he might have to wait, so he left for the day when his shift was completed.

When he got home that evening, his mind was so consumed with the intention of calling the police, that he was thrown off initially by the complete darkness he found in his hallway. The new light bulb McTeague had installed had completely blown. Grady was also breathing heavily from his walk home, a condition which had been worsening more and more lately. Groping in the darkness, he inched his way along the wall to where he knew the light fixture was. He felt with his hand for the dead bulb to unscrew it, but nearly cut his hand in doing so. All that was left were shards as the bulb had completely exploded, perhaps due to excessive wattage or faulty installation. Grady was not sure what it was. Maybe it was the overall result of a decaying building that had seen its better days.

"Darn," he muttered to himself.

He felt some glass crunch under his feet as he approached his apartment. Once inside, he turned on his own light, opened the window to let in the San Francisco air, and sat down on his couch in exhaustion. Something was wrong. His labored breathing was surfacing after expending less and less effort each day. He would definitely make an appointment with a doctor soon. But first things first. He turned on the television set and then looked down at the telephone. After recovering his breath and then taking a drink from a bottle of alcohol, he picked up the receiver. He took a deep breath before speaking:

"Yea, I wanna report somethin'," he said directly, but without urgency, to the officer at the other end of the phone.

Robotically, the officer did not hesitate to ask follow up questions: "What's the problem? Tell me about it, sir. What do you want to report? What happened and where did it happen?"

Grady took another swallow from his drink, gulping it down before going on further. "You know that Chen murder?" he now said more humbly, now that he was actually uttering the victim's name. "The Chinese fella killed downtown a few weeks ago?"

"Chen murder?" the officer said, having apparently forgotten the details of that investigation as it had actually been a month since the crime occurred. "Oh that case," the officer said, recovering himself, and a little more excited now. "What do you know about that?"

"I saw it. I was there, and I think know the man responsible."

The officer asked Grady if he could come down to the Hall of Justice on Bryant Street immediately to give a statement. When Grady described that this might involve some difficulty because of his age and inability to locate the proper bus on such short notice, the officer immediately offered to send over a squad car to pick him up and deliver him.

Grady, suddenly feeling a little agitated by the genie he had just let out of the bottle, had no choice but to agree. He sensed that there was about to be a major disruption in his life that was now unavoidable. But this had been long overdue, and he hoped that God would not punish him for carrying around his truth for so long.

The officer, who now panted with a kind of exuberance over what he had heard, said that the squad car would be over within the next twenty minutes. He told Grady, who quietly gave his address, not to leave his apartment. Grady agreed and, after hanging up his phone, he took another drink and went over to his open window to get some air. The air was still less inviting than usual. The San Francisco air now seemed more realistic and less whimsical and seductive. It was just air now.

When the police arrived, it was not a marked squad car, but two detectives instead. One was white, a young man. The other was black, a more seasoned veteran. They explained that since the case had been pursued so vigorously and was of such a high profile, that they wanted to respond to any and all information as soon and as directly as possible.

The black cop was one of the lead investigators. The young man answered to the older one, though he seemed to be capable on his own. Two marked squad cars did arrive eventually, and they parked outside of Grady's building.

With the mild commotion, Lorraine came out of her apartment to see what was going on across the hall. But Grady told her that everything was all right and that he would explain things to her later.

When the two detectives were squarely inside Grady's home, they examined the place thoroughly with their eyes and they touched a few items, before they started to pepper the old man with questions.

The black policeman, Detective Owens, started to ask questions first while the younger, Detective Frank, kept sensory track of the premises. A single uniformed officer also eventually entered the apartment.

"Am I gonna be able to go to work tomorrow?" Grady could not help but ask, before the questioning began in earnest. "I got to be there at eight."

"We don't know that yet," Owens said. "That depends. Now why did you wait so long to report this? Officially that's not a crime, but a good lawyer might be able to come up with something against you. That was a pretty stupid thing to do. A lot of people were concerned over this case. You know that. You must have seen the news."

"I was scared," Grady said initially, sticking to a reason he had considered a long time ago, shortly after witnessing the crime. "And I didn't want to get involved."

"Why didn't you want to get involved?" the young white officer asked abruptly, and from behind Grady, out of his eyesight.

"Because it was none of my business. It had to do with rich people. That's their business." Grady could not avoid it, but he felt himself becoming more honest the more he talked. "You got your world and I got mine. Plus, I was scared, like I said."

The police found themselves taken aback by what they had just heard. They had heard of such reasoning before, but never involving such an extravagant, high profile case. This was not an average street crime involving local criminals, and a person who did not want to get involved.

But as provocative as Grady's reason had been, Detective Owens did not know how to pursue it. It was something that would have to be left for the lawyers, so he decided to stick with the facts. The young cop, on the other hand, was unable to hold back.

"So you don't like rich people. Is that what you're saying? You were making some kind of protest statement against rich people. Is that it? All the while, you just decided to let a man die. That's kind of cruel, don't you think?"

Grady did not answer; he just sat, looking worn and unhappy about all the things he might have to go through in the near future. He was also feeling agitated, a little fatigued, and genuinely guilty for the first time in a while.

"So go over what happened again," Owens said, eager to get to the bottom of things.

Grady explained everything from the beginning until the end. But it was when he got to the part that he believed he had recently seen the man responsible for the crime in his building, that both detectives became more interested, though each tried to play it cool. "You didn't get a name?" Owens asked.

"No," Grady said. "But I know where he went, and he had that accent."

"What kind of accent?" the younger cop asked.

"I'm not sure, but he did say 'mate,'" Grady said.

"That could be Australian," Detective Frank said, so enthusiastically that one might believe that he had solved the case simply based on someone's way of speaking. "It could also be from New Zealand."

"But you're not sure it was him?" Owens asked, still attempting to get to the heart of the matter.

"I'm pretty sure, man," Grady said, now becoming more annoyed by the number of questions. Somehow, he believed this entire process would move along faster.

"Could you identify him if you saw him again?"

"I think so," Grady responded flatly to the black cop.

During the next ten minutes, Grady was briefed on what was going to happen next. He was going to ride down to his building with the detectives. They would take him up to East Gate Financial Services on the 9th floor where they would try to locate the man for Grady to identify. "It's late," Grady pleaded. "He might not be there. Nobody might be there. It's after building hours."

"That's all we've got right now," Detective Frank said curtly. "Even if he is not there, we are going to try and get some information about him from the owners of East Gate themselves. There may be emergency contact information in the company files, and since he spent considerable time at the building today, there is a good chance that he is well known to them and we might be able to get more than a name. We might also be able to get his home address. We're going to try to find him one way or another before this night is over and, if possible, we want to question him before morning. It's almost 7:30 now. Some people do work late. Let's go."

Before he knew it, Grady found himself in the back seat of an unmarked police cruiser that was flanked by marked cars to the front and rear. It was a scene he could not have envisioned himself in just a day ago. It was surreal. Curious tenants in the building looked out their apartment windows into the street to see what the commotion was.

"You ok pops?" said Spike, who had his door open before Grady and his police escort left the building.

"I'm fine. Nothing to worry about. Talk to you later."

Spike, the former Hell's Angel biker and gang member, looked over the police with a gloating confidence, to show that he was not intimidated by them. With his bald head, beard, and multitude of tattoos, several of the police looked at Spike suspiciously. But he was not the reason why they were there, so they moved on with their business. As they left, Spike stood there not like a Hell's Angel, but like a guardian angel of some kind.

When all the cars were in place, Grady was in a small motorcade through downtown San Francisco, and as he passed by Union Square, he felt a twinge of self-importance, as if he was some kind of dignitary. These feelings were mixed in with those of guilt, resolution, embarrassment, and annoyance. They were all fighting for supremacy and each had their say at different points. When they pulled up to his building, he was told to wait in the car while the two detectives went up to the East Gate property offices.

From the car, Grady could see Marko working the guard's desk. At almost 8pm, the lobby was empty and the two officers had to show ID to get inside the building. No one, even if the area was crowded, would know that Grady was inside the car, unless they looked closely. He imagined that those walking by the sedan speculated about who was inside and why they might be entitled to such consideration. Owens and Frank came back through the lobby about 15 minutes after they went upstairs.

"Let's go," the younger detective said to Grady, ushering him from the comfort of the car's backseat. Soon Grady was walking through the lobby with the officers. He said hello to Marko as he walked by the guard desk, but that was all.

Marko looked on with mild curiosity. He wondered about Grady's off-duty presence in the building with police officers, but as Marko was manning the guard's desk himself at the moment, he was too busy to worry about the details. He let them all pass after Grady's low-key "hello" to him. He made a mental note to ask Grady about it later.

In the elevator ride up, Grady felt like he was in a movie, now watching himself from scene-to-scene. Also, he was beginning to feel unsure about his general human status right now: Was he now a loyal building employee, a witness, a liar, a squealer, an honest citizen, a victim, or a hero? How could he be identified and when would there be a resolution to all this?

When they exited the elevator, they were confronted by the same double glass doors of East Gate Financial Services Grady had seen earlier. The only person inside at the moment again appeared to be a receptionist, though it did not look like the same woman Grady had seen a few hours ago.

"We're looking for a man who came to this building this afternoon," Detective Owens said to the young white girl sitting behind the desk, after flashing his badge.

The girl looked overwhelmed by the number of men standing above her: Grady, the two detectives, and three uniformed officers.

Owens described the man to the young woman, who called to the back to retrieve another man who came out to greet the visitors.

The man gave his name and explained that he was one of the owners of East Gate Financial Services. The detectives gave an explanation of their late evening presence and asked if the owner was aware of the clients who came to the offices around 11:00 am that morning.

The owner said he was very aware of all the clients that came in that day, as there were very few. The man who had arrived around 11:00 am and stayed until late in the afternoon was named Jack Johansson.

Johansson had come to the office early to close a deal on the purchase of some office space in the downtown area and there had been an unexpected snag requiring him to spend the majority of the afternoon at the East Gate offices. When asked to describe the man in his own words, the owner did so, giving a nearly identical description as that which had been provided by Grady, right down to the Australian-sounding accent.

Detective Frank asked if the owner could provide them with an address and a phone number and the owner said, "Yes, of course. I also have a photo of him, if it would help,"

In minutes, a folder was produced which held a company portfolio brochure showing a smiling Jack Johansson, who had reddish hair with a beard and mustache to match.

"Is this the man you encountered in the lobby this morning?" Detective Owens directed toward Grady.

Suddenly fighting off images of the night of the murder upon seeing Johansson's picture, Grady quickly calmed himself and only answered plainly: "Um pretty sure that's him, yes," he said. Meanwhile, he found himself mesmerized by the disarming smile on the photo of the man he had seen commit such a violent attack on another human being. *It's hard to tell what's going on inside people,* he thought to himself while standing there. *People can be cruel and smile about it. That's what's so scary about today's world,* he thought additionally. If the word *diabolical* had been a part of his vocabulary, it would have entered his mind at the moment.

"Is this the man you saw attack Edward Chen down the street from here about a month ago?"

"Yep, I believe that's him," Grady again responded matter-of-factly. He did not know how else to respond. He knew what he knew.

Within 10 minutes, Grady and the officers were back in the elevator on the way back down to the lobby. Owens had radioed to someone to send what Grady believed to be squad cars to an address on Bush Street. That was where they would be headed, to confront this mysterious man of apparent Australian descent.

As they passed through the lobby, Grady gave Marko a look of both confusion and surrender as he passed by the guard station.

"Talk to ya later," was all that Marko could say dryly.

"Yea," Grady responded. "Don't worry. I'm not in any kinda trouble," he added, trying to sound and appear positive and upbeat.

The truth was that he had no idea what was going to happen next in his life.

"Well that's good," Marko responded through an equally dry and weak, but sympathetic smile. He liked Grady but his relationship with him was professional and not personal, and what was going on with Grady at the moment looked very personal.

Other people in the lobby also looked on at the contingent, noting the brisk walks, darkish clothing, and shining badges. Grady was herded back into the police car as a potential witness to one of the city's biggest recent crimes.

Back inside the car, without saying a word to Grady, the two detectives pulled from in front of the office building onto Market, then to Geary and Franklin, and then over the Pine, where they made a left turn. They were followed closely by the two marked squad cars. They raced up hilly Pine Street at a fast pace with their lights on, but with no sirens. Looking into the faces of the people on the street, Grady wondered what they might be thinking as he observed them holding their coffee cups, briefcases, or leashed pets, while wearing suits or running outfits. They may have thought someone important was passing by.

But their curiosity would be only momentary. San Franciscans, in general, did not dawdle too long over serious matters. They liked to play most and reserved most of their energies for that. In fact, the more serious the matter, the greater the aversion to it for much of San Francisco's "live and let live" attitudes.

At Webster Street, the small motorcade made a left turn and then another left turn a block later onto Bush Street. From there, Grady knew the suspect's address exactly, for upon making the turn, he could see the entire block between Webster and Buchanan sealed off by another half-dozen squad cars. It looked like a siege was about to take place and he started to feel really nervous for the first time, for look what he had created. He hoped he was right about this man. Could he have been wrong? He would know soon, because if the man was at home, they would most likely be bringing him out within moments. The street was quiet otherwise, a fact that Grady also noticed.

It was a residential neighborhood populated by young professionals, many of whom probably worked downtown, in areas near Grady's own building. Some would walk to work, others would take the bus, and others still would ride a bike. They would think it their civic and social responsibility to keep their cars at home while they found environmentally-friendly ways to get to their jobs. In Grady's own neighborhood, the presence of more than one police car would have brought many people to their windows and quite a few out into the street to see what was happening. But apparently, in somewhat wealthy neighborhoods like this one, it wasn't that way.

Grady pondered this irony. Were they so used to having squad cars surround a neighbor's house that they didn't come out to look? Grady gave a slight chuckle as he considered this. Did they think it was just impolite to watch police actions? Maybe they just did not care, especially if such activity did not concern them. *Were they so wealthy that they were simply above crime and danger in the world?* Grady also considered this.

It was getting near to 8:30 in the evening and the sun, while still out, was going down fast. For the short term, there was enough light for Grady to see everything. There was a policeman directing traffic on the street and a few cars did slow to see what was happening.

The car Grady was in pulled up on Laguna, went up a half block, then turned around and parked at the intersection facing Japantown. This was where they would be when the police would bring out the individual, Grady believed.

"Johansson," Detective Owens said, trying to get out the name of the man he had been given by East Gate Services. "Jack Johansson. Are you going to recognize him if we bring him out?" he asked Grady.

"I hope so man," Grady said, trying to loosen up and establish a familiarity with the black officer. "If it's the same man, I will. But I will need to see his face again -- close up?"

"That's what this is all about, that's why we're here," the cop said, and both detectives exited the vehicle, leaving Grady alone for the first time since being in his apartment, now several hours ago.

A uniformed officer was posted outside the vehicle for Grady's safety and to keep track of him, but Grady was at least alone with his own thoughts, though he was having a hard time concentrating. To keep his head from spinning, he tried to focus himself. He forced himself to think of more practical matters, along the lines of when all this would be over, and what he might do then.

As his mind wandered over the landscape of practicality and pragmatism, it eventually found its way again to the idea of the reward, which he had yet to think about throughout the current ordeal. He believed that the reward was real now and it would be deserved, no matter what anyone said. They could not find this person without his help, after all, regardless of the delay.

However, as the evening progressed and the sun declined, Grady felt a gloom settle over himself just as darkness was settling over the neighborhood and the city. The cops had been in the shrubbery-shrouded house where Johansson apparently lived for a half hour and Grady started to run out of things to think about and ponder.

After another 45 minutes, he looked out his window to the right and he finally saw three figures moving toward him. The tallest man was in the middle. When they got closer, he saw clearly that the tall man in the middle was the man he had come to identify.

Owens and Frank were on either side of him, but they were not being aggressive with the man as police sometimes can be, like with Arthur Grant over in Oakland. This man, not handcuffed, yet suspected of murder, seemed to be walking with them as if he were one of them. Shortly, the three made a quick pivot to the front of the car, never letting Grady and the man make eye contact. Owens sat Johansson on the car's hood with his back to Grady, while Frank opened the car door and turned on the headlights.

"All right Mr. Jonas, this is going to be just like a line up. You've seen those before, right?" he said to Grady calmly and matter-of-factly. "We're going to walk him in front of the car. The beams will be in his eyes, so he won't be able to see you. But you'll get a good look at him. We'll keep him out there as long as it takes."

Frank was so direct, resting at the top of the backseat and peering right down into Grady's face, that Grady could only nod mechanically in response. He found himself quietly impressed by Detective Frank's directness and efficiency. Frank's confidence, in fact, gave Grady confidence that he was doing the right thing. After leaving the car, Detective Frank immediately joined his partner.

Grady observed closely as the suspect was turned to face the car. It had been dark that night in the street, but Grady had gotten a close look at the attacker then. This time Johansson was not wearing a coat of any kind, but a gray sweater and what appeared to be some kind of dark, heavy cotton pants. But all Grady needed was to see the distinctive eyebrows, the hair, and to get a measure of the man's height, and he was certain that they had the right individual, the one he had seen the night of the attack and murder.

"Thas him," he murmured quietly to himself, to cover a bit of righteous indignation. For in that moment, he was actually happy that justice had been done and a criminal had been caught.

After a few minutes, Frank walked over to the car again and opened the door.

"That is him," Grady said without waiting to be asked. "Um sure of it. You don't even have to ask me."

"You are sure, Mr. Jonas?" Detective Frank asked anyway. "Because this man told us that he was in England the night Mr. Chen was killed. He's very confused and says that he can prove where he was. So, Mr. Jonas, I need to ask you again if you are sure. Because if you are, we have to take him in right now. That also means that your life could change a whole lot in the near future. Do you understand everything I am saying here?"

For the first time Grady noticed that the aggressive young detective had a military-looking stare, and he was staring directly at Grady, like he was giving him an order. Grady still appreciated his sincerity because it still inspired confidence that he needed. He felt that Frank was on his side and interested in getting at the truth and putting this behind all of them. That suited Grady well at this point too. He wanted to get this all over with as well.

"I am tellin' you that's him," Grady reiterated with more vigor than before. "This is the third, fourth time I seen this man. I'm tellin' you that's who I saw yesterday and who I saw that night in the street. I can't forget those eyebrows, and that hair either. He kinda looks like the devil, don't you think."

Frank ignored this comment though, in favor of the facts.

"Ok fine, let's get going, then. We need to get you out of here before the media gets here.

PI is gonna have to tell them something since this case has been so big in the community. Everybody wants to know. But one more thing for you, I just think I should let you know. When we get down to Bryant Street, this man's lawyer is probably gonna be there. This man probably also has ties to his embassy here and he says he can prove where he was the night of the crime. This means that he might not spend much time in holding, if any. He's got a pretty wife and lives in a good San Francisco neighborhood and right now, it's your word against his. Do you understand what I'm saying at here?"

Before Grady could answer, there was a hard rapping on the hood of the car that, for a moment, jarred both Grady and the young cop. It was Owens. He was becoming impatient.

"Be right out," Frank said, after sticking his head outside the car door.

When he left, Grady was alone inside the car again. Now it was as if he were watching a television show, with all its actors and characters in place. He could clearly see the scene unfolding outside the car. For him, he ascertained, it was all over. It was up to the police now to put this man in jail, and Grady was sure he had identified the right person. However, maybe Grady's role was not completed.

Would he not have to testify if it got that far, being the only *real* witness? He could deal with this, especially if the reward might be coming his way. How did it all work? What was the timeline for the reward? Would the man actually have to be in jail before the money was given out, or did it all result from some private arrangement between the family of the victim and the suspect's identifier? Grady was seized by a sharp jolt of greed, a brief convulsion like the ones that sometimes jolted the city in the form of minor earthquakes.

To absolve his temporary guilt over his present thinking, he had to tell himself that it did not really matter in the end. He could survive without the money. He had until now. And his family? They had survived too. Maybe not under the best circumstances, but they had survived. That was better than a lot of people could say.

He would think about the reward later, but if it did not come, he could not risk losing sleep over something he had never had before anyway. He forced himself to focus again on the here and now, the reasonable and the practical. When would the present events come to an end? Was he going to work tomorrow? He could. It was getting close to 9:30 pm, with plenty of time to get home, get some sleep, and get up early.

As he thought, he watched them walk Johansson back to his home. The man did not appear rattled. He seemed very cooperative and he never looked back in the direction of the car, seeming to ensure the old man's anonymity.

Owens came back by himself and Grady could not determine what had happened to Frank. "Ok man, listen," Owens said directly as soon as he got into the driver's seat of the car. He was direct in a different way than Detective Frank was, and he turned back to face Grady. His tone was suddenly one of familiarity, trying to get through to Grady on the level of a fellow black man. "You have to come downtown with us to give an official statement. Based on your eyewitness account, we are going to bring this man in. He's calling his lawyer right now and he'll probably get out on bail before the sun rises. I don't know if he's guilty or not. But I want you to be sure you know what you are doing. You're not just doing this to get some attention or for the money, are you?"

Because of his directness, Grady could not help but to look at the detective to determine what kind of man he was. He was about 20 years Grady's junior, so he had probably been around the block himself a few times, especially being a police officer. Therefore, Grady had to respect the cynicism and the implied doubt of his honesty.

However, now frustrated and bit insulted, Grady started speaking at some length, and with some force behind his words: "Now why would I have you come all the way up here in this rich, white part of San Francisco and have you pull some man out of his house and say he killed somebody if I did not think that was true? I'm not crazy, and I already told you why I waited so long. I didn't want to get into this. Now I have gotten into it. I'm sorry it took so long. But it's a cold, nasty world out heah. Sometimes you just want to keep steppin' and mind your own business. You dig it, man? Let other people live their lives and you live your own." He declined to give any credence to the remark about the reward.

"Ok then pops," Owens said, turning on the car's engine. "Because I can't really say where all this is headed." Detective Frank returned to the car within the next five minutes, and they were off for downtown.

Detective Owens' last words had left an ominous tone in the car's air.

CHAPTER XIII

Grady was at the police station until about 1 am. He didn't get home until about 2 am. Between the paperwork and the interrogation, he was exhausted. The police had him go over not only every detail of the night of the crime, but on what had happened in his life since. Not only that, they also asked him some things about his past. Several more enthusiastic detectives even threatened him with arrest for withholding evidence for so long, but they could not get around his explanation that he didn't want to get involved until now. Though this frustrated them, they were forced to admit that there were no laws on the books that actually enforced the reporting of a crime of any sort, by random witnesses.

In the end, he was let go and told that they would be in contact. Though he himself had a million questions of his own, he was too tired, too overwhelmed, and a little too intimidated to ask. So, he was taken home in an unmarked squad car.

When he got to his building, he saw that his hallway was again black from the recently blown out bulb. He decided then and there that he would call in and take the approaching day off from work. He needed some time to think about recent events, and life in general.

Once inside his apartment, after groping his way through his hallway's darkness, he immediately called the building to leave a message for Tony. He was tired. The night was, now in reality, early Tuesday morning. Grady opened the window briefly just to get a sense of what might be going on outside in the streets. It was relatively quiet for San Francisco, even though it was a warm night.

Warm or not, the air still did not provide him the same comfort and confidence it had in recent weeks. Because of his recent experiences, his soul was occupied elsewhere, somewhere now outside the city's reach.

During the night, Grady slept quietly for the most part, awakened briefly only by a dream. In the dream, his grandson Paulie sat on a pier and looked out onto an expanse of water. The small black boy appeared to be the only person in the world and master of all that he surveyed. But he did not appear lonely or afraid; on the contrary, he looked at peace in his solitude.

He was wearing all white and the water, which Grady assumed to be the San Francisco Bay as it stretched out from Hunter's Point, was bluish green and clear. Then, and this is what woke Grady up, a white man dressed in a white gown came toward the pier where little Paulie sat. He was floating over the waters. His hair was brown and the closer he got, the faster he moved toward Paulie. Sensing danger in the dream, with an impending collision between the floating white man and the peaceful black boy, Grady somehow forced himself to wake up, to prevent what he deemed through his subconscious to be a potentially disastrous conflict. He awoke flustered, but almost immediately went back to sleep.

When he awoke in the morning, he had forgotten about the dream completely. If he had had a chance to reflect over the nocturnal events, he might have seen some revelations and solutions in the imagery.

Reality invaded his life early that morning, as it often did, for when he turned on the television set, the lead story focused on the arrest of a suspect in the "Street Rage" murder. There were no pictures of Johansson, only the morning reporter lustfully detailing the news of a purported capture. Grady sat and watched, without the need to hurry for work. The ball was now rolling; the world was now handling its businesses, with a little help from him. He wanted to sit back and watch and see how things would develop from here, not *fully* realizing that he was now an integral part of it all.

The reporter, a thin and energetic young Asian woman, whom Grady had seen on the TV many times before, said that the police, acting on a tip, had made an arrest and that there would be a news conference to provide more information around noon. The only people interviewed were the Chens, including Edward Chen's wife, Jennifer, and his parents, who looked disheveled at the door of their home in the Richmond District avenues. There was no mention at all of the reward in this early report. But since he had the day off, Grady would wait around for the news conference. The police had also said that they might contact him again today, so that was a double reason why it was good for him to stay close to home today, which was a day off anyway.

His name had not been mentioned by the reporter. That made him feel good, as he still wanted to preserve some anonymity. Maybe the newspaper had more information than the TV, he thought, so he decided to go out quickly before making breakfast and get one to read. Presently, he could not avoid the idea of the reward in his mind.

Closing his window, he also could not deny that all of a sudden life had become exciting. Perhaps he should have come forward long ago. It was nice to be a part of something larger than himself. Perhaps this was what he had been missing in his life in recent years, where he had become a bit of hermit living in San Francisco's Tenderloin. Perhaps he needed to be recognized in some way. Being recognized removed an edge from his life, it seemed. He had more energy overall this morning.

On the way out and down the stairs of his building, meanwhile, he heard vulgar sounds coming from Lorraine's apartment. The sounds were familiar enough to any adult mind, but he dismissed them in favor of his own concerns. He had an ongoing suspicion as to what might be going on in his neighbor's apartment; but, like the Chen murder, he resolved to let that situation unfold on its own as well, as he had even less stake in it.

"That woman is too bold," was all he managed to say to himself regarding Lorraine, as he skipped down the stairs.

Walking down the street, however, his mood changed again and suddenly he did not feel that much differently than he did yesterday. All he had done was relieve a burden, but his life was still the same, was it not? He saw the same faces and observed the same activities and still had the same problems. Perhaps the reward would add new dimensions to life that would eliminate all his daily malaise for good.

Somehow, he had not expected the police to buy the excuse for not reporting the crime sooner. But they were so happy to get the information, to clear up the case, that there seemed to be no real hard feelings, with the exception of a few officers. Jennifer Chen and her parents were happy for the apparent closure and Grady had to admit that he was happy to see that consequence.

They had suffered and had been victims. He now felt sympathy for them and, for the first time, the word "Samaritan" entered his mind, in reference to himself. It was the word that the pastor had used and the description of that Biblical account of *The Good Samaritan,* which he had heard in church, poured more into Grady's mind as he walked to get the newspaper. His actions, late though they were, had succeeded in helping others. He had been a "good Samaritan" in his own way, though deep down he still wanted the reward money also.

In the newspaper, which he read when he got back to his apartment, there were again substantially more details about the case than what he had seen on the television. The story ran on the front page, with a big banner across the top of the front, that read: ***Suspect Arrested in Month-Old 'Street Rage' Murder.*** There were no pictures of Johansson here either, only a sharp looking picture of the late Edward Chen wearing a tie and professional looking eyeglasses, and an adjacent one of Jennifer Chen in tears.

This story read:

> Late last night, San Francisco police announced the arrest of a suspect in the death of real estate developer Edward Chen, whose body was found lying on the sidewalk at a street corner in the heart of the financial district last month. The arrest was the result of a previously unknown eyewitness who came forward.
>
> Police would offer only a few details, but a source said the suspect was an Australian national who also worked in the downtown area. Officially, police would offer no comment on this information.

"We have someone of interest. That's all we will say right now," a spokesman said. "Hopefully, for the sake of the family, we can put an end to this."

The spokesman confirmed that the arrest was the result of new information but would not provide any further details. The source within the department said that the suspect was arrested at his home on Bush Street about 9:15 last night and was identified at the arrest scene by an unidentified man who reportedly witnessed the assault on Chen. "If the witness holds up," the source said, "we think we have the right guy. But I have to admit that we are still a long way from closing this case."

Officials at San Francisco's Australian Interest Section, a branch of the Australian Consulate, would not comment on the investigation and would not speculate on the identity of the man taken into custody. The man's name was being withheld by police.

Police also would not speculate on the how the attack on Chen might have occurred, or the motive for the crime, though the source said that the witness' testimony seemed to confirm theories that the attack was, in fact, a case of so called "street rage." "Two people bumping into each other on the street," the police source said. "Things just went too far. That's modern life for you."

The witness was not identified by police for his own protection.

Family members of the victim reached by phone last night voiced their hope that the arrest would lead to a speedy resolution in the case.

"We are very happy as a family on hearing this news," Jennifer Chen, the wife of the deceased man, said in a phone call last night. "We hope that justice will be served. It has been over a month and we have been hoping that there would be some resolution."

*Asked if the person who came forward might be eligible
to receive the $100,000 reward, which has been offered by
the family and the Chinese Chamber of Commerce, Ms.
Chen said she did not see why not. "The reward was offered
for a reason. But of course we will have to follow through
and see if this suspect really is the man who murdered my
husband. The reward may be contingent upon a conviction
for the crime. But we will honor it, of course."*

Grady put the paper down in his lap. He wanted to take in the
full effect of all that he had read. But just then he heard yelling
and wild commotion outside in the hallway, which quickly
jarred his concentration. As he listened, he heard voices rising
outside his door. Some of the voices he easily determined were
being spoken in Spanish. He rushed to his door and opened it.

There he saw Lorraine, at her door, in yet another argument,
this time with what appeared to be a Hispanic woman. This
woman was apparently the Hispanic father's wife and the
situation was what Grady had suspected over the past few weeks.
The woman was looking for her husband, who was having an
affair with another woman: Lorraine. The husband, after all the
early morning altercations, was having an affair with who Grady
thought was his enemy, right in the same building, and just one
floor below his own home. What nerve, Grady thought, as he
looked through the crack in his door.

Then suddenly, bringing her verbal Spanish-language attack
to a climax, Grady witnessed the Hispanic mother physically
lunge at Lorraine, jumping on top of her and sending them both
to the floor, just inside Lorraine's doorway. Grady could not
believe what he was witnessing, and for a short time he could
see only the feet of the two women kicking and wrestling.

Grady threw open his door and immediately rushed to offer Lorraine help. As he had known her longer, he felt compelled to come to her aid the most. As Grady got to the door, the Hispanic father came rushing from a back room only partially dressed, confirming his wife's suspicions.

"*¡Dios mio!*" Grady heard him say. "*¡Marisol! ¡Parada! ¡Parada!*"

When they pulled the small, enraged woman off Lorraine, they realized that they would now have to call an ambulance. The Hispanic mother had stabbed Lorraine in the upper chest with a kitchen knife. There was only a single puncture, but it was bleeding and it was not clear exactly how deep the wound had gone.

"*¡Dios Mio!*" the Hispanic father said again as Lorraine rose to her feet. She was wearing a loose-fitting top and some jeans, and a pool of blood was now clearly forming over her wound.

"I'm fine," Lorraine muttered, however, a combination of pride and shame in her voice. She took out a cigarette and lit it, as Grady took a closer look at the assaulted area.

The Hispanic father ran to a back room to get his clothes. His wife breathed heavily, after she had moved out into the hallway, now on her feet. Her work had been done; the bloodstained, dull-bladed kitchen knife lay on the floor. The woman looked now to be in a kind of exhaustive stupor. The husband then came rushing back, disheveled, but fully dressed now.

"Go on," Lorraine said. "All of you get out of here. Enjoy your day. I'll be all right. Don't worry about me. I'll just put a little alcohol on it and wash it out. I'll be fine."

"Don't be a fool Lorraine," Grady said. "Call a doctor. You don't know how deep that is. You need to get it checked out right. I'm gonna call an ambulance right now."

"I'll be all right, I told you!" Lorraine repeated haughtily, before then morbidly taking a dip of the blood on one of her fingers and tasting it with her tongue. "I haven't tasted my own blood in a long time. Sure is dark and thick, like barbecue sauce. Hahaha! But maybe you're right…maybe I should call somebody. Never seen blood before this thick and dark. Have you?" Throughout, she wore a mischievous smile on her face. No lessons had apparently been learned by her.

"I'll call the ambulance," Grady said, ignoring her ghoulish comments, as the Hispanic couple, both with heads bowed in a kind of shared shame, made their way back up to their own apartment. There were no goodbyes or apologies, only an ignominious departure.

After making the call, Grady rushed back to find Lorraine, who was now sitting in her doorway. She had a towel to put pressure on her wound. "Thank you," Lorraine said. "But I'm not gonna press charges or anything. That wouldn't be right, would it? I mean I started the whole thing, right? These things happen. How can I go on living in this building now? I'm gonna have to watch myself from now on," she said through another mischievous smile to Grady, which showed some of her missing front teeth.

"All I can tell you is to be careful who you mess with heah," Grady said, somewhat freshly annoyed by the whole situation. "Some people can only take so much. You should know that by now." Lorraine took another drag from her cigarette, still sitting on the floor, and putting pressure on the wound.

An ambulance was there within ten minutes and she managed to walk out to it, and within 15 minutes, she was gone, laughing and joking with the attendants all the way.

Grady did not know what to make of her. Did Lorraine long for death? Was she bored with life and had to find excitement in it this way? One day she was not going to be so fortunate. There had to be more to life than just making random decisions and ruining the lives of others.

For much of the rest of the morning, all that Grady heard were arguments between the Hispanic couple upstairs. There was one brief period where there were the sounds of things breaking, but mostly it was Spanish-speaking voices at high, enraged pitches. For some fresh air and different sounds, Grady opened his widow and sat close by it. The air worked for him this morning. Perhaps the San Francisco air could also work for one if one consciously summoned and invited it, which Grady did right now, putting aside all other concerns to seek the air out directly, and this worked for him right now.

The noise finally died down about two hours after the stabbing, when one of the two upstairs neighbors raced through the hallway and apparently out of the building. Though Grady did not want to see the Hispanic family destroyed, he was relieved at the apparent end of today's conflict, which was taking up his day off from work.

Later in the afternoon, after taking a nap and getting some rest, he got the call he had been waiting for from the police, who informed him that Johansson had made bail and was now out, but that they would need to see Grady again before the day was over to get some more information. He did not know what to make of the fact that the man was out, a man who had committed a crime and had been on the loose all this time. He also felt a little put out knowing that he would have to take another trip all the way back down to the station, as it was already getting late in the day, and he was expected to return to work in the morning.

He asked the police if they could come back to his apartment for any interviews, but they said no. They needed to record any additional information officially, with the equipment they had at the station. They did, however, send over another escort.

When he got the station, Grady was introduced to an officer he had not met before, though Owens and Frank were also inside the room. He was informed that he was to be given a polygraph test.

"It's called a lie detector test," the burly, thick-necked, white-haired cop said, a bit condescendingly, as if Grady were a child. "You know what that is, don' cha'?"

"Yea, I heard of it man," Grady responded in a way to let those present know that he was annoyed by these new requirements. "But why do I have to take it? I told ya'll all I knew and what I saw, and you still act like you don't believe me."

"We believe you," the thick-faced white man said. "But this is standard procedure. Now just sit back and relax, listen to the questions carefully, and clearly respond with 'yes' or 'no.'"

Throughout the questioning, which took about a half hour, Grady was asked again, among other questions, if he was certain of what he had seen and if he was certain of the person he had identified. After it was over, he was not told if he had passed or not.

"We won't know for a few hours," Owens said. "We'll have someone take you home in a bit." Grady was relieved at this information, but found what he had been through a little strange, especially the doubting of his sincerity. He was, after all, helping them at this point.

While he was sitting in a room preparing for one final briefing from Owens, he was brought a visitor. It was Jennifer Chen. She was a lot shorter than she appeared on television. She was at the station answering questions and giving information of her own. When she had heard that Grady was there, she wanted to meet him.

She came into the room, not in the humble, bent over posture of some of the more traditional Chinese Americans still inhabiting San Francisco, but with the gait and countenance of a modern, intelligent, and confident Chinese woman. She had no trace of an accent and had a rather firm and direct handshake, particularly in contrast to her overall physical size.

Like the Chinese that went in and out of Grady's building, Jennifer Chen was of the professional class. Grady could recall when he and his wife first moved to San Francisco that the Chinese had been more humble and could be seen bowing and speaking their native language publicly. Grady and his wife had found this fascinating, coming from the both homogenous and bi-cultural South. This woman before him and her kind though were the waves of the future, bypassing blacks by leaps and bounds, in education, social status, wealth, and sophistication. Grady was not necessarily jealous, but he still could not help comparing the cultural differences and seeming inequities he witnessed more and more every day, and he felt powerless to do anything about them. *Would black people struggle forever, he had thought previously in his life?*

"I just wanted to come in and thank you for coming forward," Jennifer Chen said through a reserved smile.

"I jes' hope I was able to help you," Grady said to the woman who wore blue slacks and a matching light jacket. He decided not to detail what took him so long to come forward.

"They tell me that they want to keep your identity secret for now, but I know who you are and we'll get the reward to you as soon as this is all over. But thank you again."

This comment left him at a loss for words as he had not expected to meet his *benefactor* face-to-face, and so suddenly. He did not know whether to get excited over what she had said, or to remain humble.

Instinct told him to remain humble.

"Thank you," he said. "I'm sorry for your loss, and I hope I kin help. I hope your family kin get some peace of mind now too." Though he had ridiculed the woman for her excessive emotions just a few weeks ago, he felt sincere now. He felt he had to be.

At this juncture, he did feel for the Chen family, but he secretly wondered if this whole thing would have ever been resolved without his help. Would the wealthy and well-spoken, the powerful, and influential, with all their expertise and technology, have been able to solve the crime without the help of an old black man with only a high school diploma? He was not bitter or high-minded. He just felt he was only being practical in a world that dictated the rules to people like him.

"I'm sure your husband is in a better place right now," Grady could not help but add. "He didn't ask for what happened to him and I'm sure God teks things like that into consideration. I think God looks out fuh innuhcent people," he concluded, not really knowing for certain if Edward Chen might have had some complicity in his own death that night. In fact, Grady had never even considered who had started the fight that night: who had pushed whom first. Grady had only moved towards the altercation after he had heard the two men shouting, their voices carried by the hollow and fog-soaked San Francisco air.

That is what he had told the police. Perhaps Chen had had it coming. Grady had never really considered that. Maybe it was self-defense. However, the image of Johansson's face in his head told him differently.

"My husband was an atheist," Jennifer Chen responded to Grady's suggestion of an afterlife for the dead. "He did not believe in such things. He believed that once your life is over, then you die. That was it. That is why he tried to live his life to the fullest. But thank you for your comment and I respect your beliefs. I will be in touch through lawyers or the police department. Make sure that you remain available to them so that I can locate you."

Grady acknowledged this in an unassuming and professional way, and Jennifer Chen left the room smiling, leaving Grady momentarily alone. But Detective Owens entered right after that, and Owens did not necessarily like Grady. Grady could tell. Owens didn't care for Grady's decision to hold onto the information he had for so long and he was behind the doubt of Grady's credibility, leading to the lie detector test.

"What you going to do with that money, anyway?" Owens asked contemptuously after Jennifer Chen had gone. "I know she offered you reward money."

"Don't know yet man," Grady said, thinking that his decisions were none of Owens' business anyway. "Don't have it yet. I'll know when I get it. Money always comes in handy for something doesn't it?"

"Well you know you might not get it until a conviction and that might take a long time brother," Owens added tauntingly.

Grady looked Owens over disdainfully before responding: "I kin wait. I waited this long."

"What makes you think they going to believe an old nigger like you in this town anyway?" Owens then asked bluntly. "You lucky you got this far. We'll see what happens going forward from here. You better watch yourself, and I hope you tellin' the truth. For your sake!"

"You got somethin' to say man, then say it!" Grady responded angrily, deciding to go on the offensive, even glaring back at the officer.

"I think you know what I'm saying," Owens said.

Grady knew that he could get only so haughty with a police officer, who had all the power, whether he was black like Grady or not. But Grady could not hold back.

"Let's put it this way," Grady said, feeling more assertive now. "I'm all you got. Yea, I took my time comin' forward. But if they don't want me, that's up to them. If they would ratha have the white man go free, that's up to them too? He'll just go back to Germany or Canada or wherever he's from and you'll never hear from him again, and he might even kill somebody else. Or maybe he'll just stay here and keep workin' and tell his friends back home that he came over here and killed somebody in the streets and just got away with it. If he gets away with killin' somebody, what else will he do?"

Owens only smirked at Grady's hypothetical narrative and new aggressiveness. "Go ahead man," Owens said before leaving. "Get out of here and go home. We know where you are and we will be in touch." An officer entered the room within moments to drive Grady home.

He got back around 6 pm on what was now a Tuesday, and he knocked on Lorraine's door to check on her but there was no answer. The silence made Grady worry a little. But he had to get ready for work in the morning. He decided after work tomorrow he would check on her again.

In the evening, he opened his window. He wondered what was happening to the world, to humanity. He had certainly not lived a perfect life, but now that he had decided to do something "good," his individual actions had somehow set the world's shortcomings in sharp relief. He had even seen one neighbor stab another. He had been a witness to that crime also, not until now even recognizing the parallels between the two. But this one was different. Lorraine didn't seem to even care that she had been attacked, and the Hispanic couple might simply resume their lives again. He wasn't sure. Maybe he had to get out of the Tenderloin altogether.

The air from outside buffeted Grady's face as he thought about these things. He smelled automobile exhaust and other stenches from the alley beneath him. He could recognize the differences. But with a quick breeze, the smells were temporarily evicted, and he inhaled and got some fresher material into his lungs. It felt good, like breathing in new life from the city itself, and the air was cooler today. San Francisco never lost its ability to occasionally mesmerize and tranquilize.

Ironically, the same city that had produced the crimes he had witnessed, still somehow sustained him. But was it the city itself, or was it God that sustained him? Had not God created the city in which he dwelt, even one as notorious for so much as San Francisco? Who then was in charge, God, the city, or the individual? Indeed, what forces controlled his very own life? In recent years, he had thought that he controlled his life, compared to his early years in the South, where his environment seemed to be in control. But who or what was in control now? All of a sudden, he felt like a puppet in life again, controlled by forces that he could not always see necessarily or even converse with and question. As he looked out the window and breathed in the air, this line of thinking became overwhelming to him, and he just wanted the simplicity of going to work again, so he closed the window to get ready for the next day. The consistency and reliability of the work environment would be the balm that would soothe all of his current anxieties, though he knew that his part in the police investigation was far from concluded. Detective Owens had made that clear, and there was also still the reward of course!

Returning to work the next morning, no one made any mention of the crime or the arrest in the Edward Chen murder. The lack of discussion on what had become such a public story was a bit puzzling to him and part of him felt the need to broach the subject with someone. Only Big Eric made passing mention of the crime and arrest and only jokingly, when he asked out loud in the lobby what took the San Francisco police department so long to catch the guy.

Grady had wanted to jump in and respond, but managed to restrain himself. He did not even bring it up at lunch with Walter and Wizard. He felt, "what was the use." Instead, the three talked about their missing friend, Bill, whom Walter had not seen in almost three weeks now.

"Have ya' called the police?" Grady asked.

"Kall de pulice," a surly Walter asked, unlike his usual, more humbler self. "Wut dey gon'do fuh me? Um gon ask about uhnothuh missin' homeless man?

"Was wrong with you today?" Grady asked, as Wizard laughed hollowly out loud into the air at Walter's apparent abrupt change in character. People walking the streets looked over at Wizard's strange sounds.

Wizard was amused that Walter had somehow verified his own cynical view of mankind. "He has been behaving that way lately," Wizard said calmly now, with a coffee cup to his lips, looking now more like a mannered statesman than the eccentric, street person that he was well known to be. "And it doesn't have to do with Bill's disappearance either. He's been getting like that in general lately. Don't you know that we live in an age of anxiety now, and it's sucking us all into it like a vacuum, even those like your mild-mannered friend here."

"He ull turn up soon enuf," Walter said, seeking to reclaim the optimism that Wizard said he had apparently allowed the world to temporarily steal. "But I don' need to kull no police. Uh tell you dat rat now."

Grady did not feel like arguing. He had no idea where Bill could be and could not even guess. He was not really part of that world, the world of the street people – not anymore. Perhaps Bill went back to Oregon where he said he was from originally and did not feel that he was under any obligation to let anyone know he was leaving.

"Well, I got to be getting back," Grady said, feeling turned off by Walter's new grumbling tone and Wizard's smug cynicism. Leaving and walking back to the office, he wondered if their friendship might be coming to an end. He did not want to give up on his friends. Perhaps it was just a mood they were going through, similar to his own moods. Everyone seemed to be going through them these days. Maybe Wizard was right. But now that Bill was missing, Grady hoped that the absence would not destroy the relationship he had established with his little group.

By nine o'clock Wednesday night, Grady had drunk three quarters of a bottle of red wine he had gotten. He was borderline drunk, and he was feeling brave and free. By ten o'clock, the bottle was gone.

As he sat on his couch, still having to work the next day, some light San Francisco winds blew through the window he had left open. By eleven, he was asleep on his couch, still wearing his clothes, with the frantic lights from the television providing his apartment a strobe effect.

Around midnight, Grady experienced a dream about black preachers at a black church in front of a rousing black congregation. It was a larger-scale version of the scene he had experienced at the service with Evangeline Bishop. The dream though ended when the drunken and weary Grady miraculously woke up after hearing a subtle noise outside his window, coming from his fire escape.

CHAPTER XIV

Except for the flickering TV lights, the apartment was dark, and when Grady turned toward his open window after hearing the noise, he was certain that he saw the figure of a human being fully opening his window. Groggy from sleep and the bottle of wine he had finished, an instinct told him to use the remote control and turn the television off so that complete darkness and knowledge of his apartment might give him some kind of advantage. As soon as he did this, the figure stormed into the apartment, hitting the floor.

Grady did not know whether to cry out in protest or run and hide. He did not fashion himself a coward, but he was not necessarily a physical fighter either. If asked, he would most likely classify himself as an individual who would fight or defend what was his if his back was against the wall. He knew he would protect what was his own. He might even die for it.

In the dark right now, he felt angry and offended that someone would enter his own living space. But, cognizant of his age, and his mental and physical vulnerability, he decided to make his way to his bathroom in silence, instead. Sober, and in the light of day, he might have resorted to a physical altercation, win or lose.

Right now though, he managed to make it inside his bathroom safely and lock the door, though just getting up quietly from his couch took some effort. He was still technically inebriated, despite the adrenaline now flowing through him. However, once inside the bathroom, he heard footsteps inside his apartment. He wanted to yell out of anger at the intruder's boldness, but he thought it perhaps better not to let the person know of his whereabouts. He saw a light turn on through the crack under the bathroom door.

"I know you're in there old man," a voice said from outside the bathroom door. "I don't want to hurt you. I just want to straighten you out about a few things." The male voice sounded around the mid-30s in age to Grady and it also sounded educated and white. Living in San Francisco, with its celebrated cultural diversity, had also accustomed him to a wide variety of voices and speech patterns over the years.

The man, whomever he was, had found Grady out, and was suddenly right outside the bathroom door, only a few feet away. Grady did not move or say anything inside the bathroom, which provided a lot of space for the amount of rent he paid. He sat up against the door, bracing it with his back. He did not believe that the intruder could gain entry, but Grady also knew that he was still drunk and he did not want his decisions dictated by a bottle of wine. So he stayed still and stayed quiet.

Sitting there, he subsequently heard the man start to break and smash things inside the apartment. Grady wanted to fight back, but couldn't. He knew that a confrontation might lead to violence and a fight with younger man that he might not be able to win, so he continued to bluff his presence inside the bathroom. For the first time in some years, he engaged in a direct prayer to God for deliverance in this situation and overall peace in this life. While he prayed, objects continued to smash, including what he believed to be his television set.

The carnage was over after about seven minutes, during which time Grady nearly dozed off because of the heady wine.

The man returned to the door. "They're going to call you in to testify before a grand jury soon, old man. When you come out of that bathroom and see this place, I want you to think long and hard about what you're gonna say when they call you. You get my meaning? Because I'll be back. The next time, you might get to know that alley down there up close. You got that? This is more than a threat." The door was then kicked so severely that it forced Grady's head to bump up against it.

"I'll be watching you and I will come back," the man added, "and remember: you don't know who I am. But we know who you are."

After that there were the sounds of walking away, stepping on broken objects, and then the sounds of clanging metal. The man apparently was walking down the fire escape to the street.

What would have happened had he not been able to make it to the bathroom, Grady thought as he slowly rose to his feet. He was still wary of going outside to see his apartment, but he had to go. He was not sure whether he was going to call the police or not.

At first, he opened the door slowly, and then as he got a view of the carnage, he thrust the door open angrily. The light was still on, the window was wide open, and a cold wind was blowing in from the outside. It chilled him to the bone. He walked over to the window first to look down into the alley. There was no one in sight. The lever to the metal fire escape had been pulled and the contraption still reached down to the street.

Having recovered his senses somewhat, he decided that he would pull the fire escape back up to his level after looking over his apartment. It was about as bad as he had heard. The television had indeed been smashed. There was a hole in the screen, and it had been tossed to the side of the room where the front door was. There were broken dishes, glasses, and sofa cushions strewn about, and the refrigerator was lying on its side.

Thinking as he looked around, and as anger began to build within him, Grady decided not to call 911, but he would try and call Owens or Frank about what had happened specifically, especially since he suspected this invasion of his home was related to the Chen investigation.

He had not heard anything about a grand jury. He was not even exactly sure what a grand jury did. What he felt though was that someone had found out he was the witness and now he was being threatened. As a result of these thoughts, he currently found himself angry and afraid at the time. It was the anger that enabled him to focus.

As he started to clean up the apartment, Grady wondered if it had all been worth it to report what he had seen. "Shoulda just kept my mouth shut and said nothin' to nobody," he mumbled to himself as he picked up some pillow cushions.

After cleaning up and struggling to crank the fire escape back up to his level, he had to stop for shortness of breath. It was the same shortness of breath he felt walking up the hill to his daughter's, and which he had been feeling from time to time lately in general. He then called the SFPD to try and reach one of the detectives. By this time, it was 2 am and his brain had sobered significantly from the alcohol. He asked for Owens first. Even though he did not necessarily like the man, Owens was still a middle-aged black man and Grady felt that a connection on race and age-levels might yield him more progress. But Owens wasn't there.

It was a long shot that either detective would be there, it being so late, but Grady asked, and the young white cop, Frank, *was* there in fact. At first the desk sergeant thought Grady was a crank caller, but Grady put forth a brief tirade and the sergeant put him through to the young cop. In the process, Grady had to explain that he had been a witness to a crime and that he had recently been threatened and had his apartment vandalized because of it, he believed.

"Detective Frank," the young officer said, sounding as brisk and official at 2:30 am, as he did at noon. After Grady explained what had happened, Frank insisted on sending over a unit to look into things, saying that the department might need to collect evidence, if indeed there was some connection between what had happened, and the Chen murder suspect, Johansson.

The way he put it, Grady had no choice. The old man had thought about working in the morning, but police in his apartment again, for forever how long, might definitely eliminate that possibility.

As the conversation moved forward, Grady learned for a fact that events had been moving along without his knowledge.

"Yes, a grand jury may meet in two to three weeks because Mr. Chen's business had some dealings with the federal government. That is possible," Frank admitted. "We would certainly contact you in that case, but the fact that the intruder knew about it means that someone knows you are a witness."

Grady felt his heart beat a little faster at this admission. His emotions were again somewhere between mild fear and anger, this time over not having been informed about the most recent developments involving the case.

"Well why don't you tell me the whole story *detective*," a surly, frustrated Grady demanded, his wine-soaked brain still trying to completely recover itself. "Spell it out for me please."

"Johansson has been very cooperative, Mr. Jonas. He's not going anywhere. He still claims that he was in England the night Edward Chen was killed. We checked his alibi by phone and it checked out clean. To be sure though, we had to send some investigators to London to conduct interviews. All this will take some time, but based on everything else we have—some things which I cannot get into with you—we may have enough to present to a grand jury sooner rather than later. How your intruder knew all this is interesting, to say the least.

"This is why I want to send someone over there immediately and if I were you, at least for the weekend, I would consider staying somewhere else. I really don't think that you are in any danger now, but I would consider it. Whoever it was just wanted to send you a message. If you stay somewhere over the weekend, that will give us the chance to talk about getting you into protective custody early next week. Just let us know where you will be if you leave. For now, Mr. Jonas, let the officers come over there and look over the apartment. It may take them at least an hour to evaluate the scene."

Grady agreed to let the officers over to investigate the break-in to his apartment. While he waited for them he thought about calling in again to be off the next day because he did not know exactly how long the police might take in his apartment this time. But when he considered what had happened to Buddy when Tony had gotten fed up with his work habits, he decided to try to make it to work in the morning, no matter what time he went to bed.

While he waited for the police, Grady also thought about where he might stay for the next few days. His daughter came to mind. The thought of staying with his daughter in San Francisco's black ghetto, was not exactly enticing, but it would be just for the weekend. However, maybe it would be nice to spend some time in an all-black environment for a change, to see what that was like again. He had not done it in a while. In some ways, it might be like returning to the womb, although this womb could be polluted by despair, poverty, depression, drug addiction, and high crime. Still, he would be insulated from the situation he was in now. Current circumstances seemed to be forcing him back into his cultural and ethnic origins.

He called Detective Frank back, hoping he would still be there. "I got an address where I'll be the next couple days" Grady told him and he was assured by the young officer that "Everything will be all right."

Several officers invaded Grady's apartment thirty minutes later, staying for a little over an hour. One took pictures, while two others asked Grady questions, and a fourth examined the scene for clues and evidence. When they left at 4:30 am, Grady tried to get some sleep.

By 6:30, he was up and getting dressed for work. He had gone on this little amount of sleep before, but it had been a while. Surprisingly, he thought to himself as he got dressed for work, that he did not feel that bad. He thought he could get through the day on extra coffee and constant movement.

His apartment, meanwhile, remained in mild disarray over what happened the night before. He would clean it up completely after work and before he went over to his daughter's.

One problem he did not have on this morning was noisy neighbors. Since the altercation with Lorraine and the Hispanic family, he had not heard much at all from the upper floor or across the hall. He still had not checked on Lorraine, but would have to do so after the weekend at his daughter's.

He wondered as he walked to work how he was going to explain to his daughter that he wanted to stay with her over the weekend, and how she would react. He would call her from work and hoped that her phone bill was paid, and her phone was working. This would be an unusual request from him, and he might have to explain to some extent why he was making it. He did not believe she would mind since he was only staying for a couple nights at the most.

When he got to the building, he thought that he might feel relieved, but he felt the opposite. As soon as he saw Tony and realized that he would have to stand behind the desk most of the day, he started to feel queasy and unsettled. *This is going to be a long one,* he thought. If he could just get through it, everything would be all right.

Before taking his post, he asked Tony if he could run down and get his second cup of coffee of the morning. He did not generally drink that much coffee, and having more than two cups would be beyond his limit. Still, he felt that he needed at least one more. He had sobered up overnight, but a full bottle of wine took its time to vacate the system, especially with only two hours of sleep. With a second cup of coffee in hand, he walked back up to the desk.

Throughout the morning, he took measured sips. It worked and he started to feel better. As soon as Tony left on rounds, he decided to place a quick call to his daughter before she got on her way for the day. Fortunately for him, she was there and agreed that he could stay there over the weekend.

He told her that he just wanted to get away and how he had enjoyed the waters when he was over there the last time. He said he would pack a bag when he got home from work and catch the bus over there before it got too dark. He did not tell her anything else that was going on in his life. He did not want to worry her or have her asking a lot of questions. He was not looking forward to walking up the steep hill to get to her apartment, however.

"Hello my dear," said a voice from out of his view as he stood at the security desk, pondering the events in his life. It was Evangeline Bishop, who he had not seen since the church service on Sunday.

"I've been watching for you," she added. "I guess we keep missing each other. Have you been all right? Henry asked about you. He was wondering when you might be coming back to join us. The pastor asked too. Henry asked again whether you might consider becoming a deacon at the church. We need more men."

Grady felt a warmth in her words, which reminded him of the service. Both her words and the church service were soothing, honest, and sincere, though he had not had much chance to actually recall the details of the service in recent days.

To Grady, Evangeline remained decent in an increasingly indecent world. Her makeup and dress were simple, but powerful in their simplicity, like Grady remembered women used to dress in the old days. Her goodness was so powerful that Grady felt a brief spasm in his soul at that moment to confess all his sins to her, but he quickly considered that their present environment would make that impossible.

But she brought back the serenity of the church service and it became clear to him the impact she was having in his life. She was like some kind of spiritual beacon, beckoning him to repentance and righteousness. Right now, her request made the thought of returning to the church sound enticing. As a deacon, he would be able to do something dignified and worthwhile. He might be able to feel *clean* again. Still he hesitated, because he was unsure how to respond exactly, his mind also buffeted by the current events in his life.

"A deacon?" he smirked in a self-deprecating way. "I think you might have the wrong man."

"The wrong man?" she said quickly. "There are no wrong men. God can work with anyone. Just give him a chance."

"I guess that's true," Grady admitted. "He's the potter and we are the clay. Isn't that what they say?" he added, remembering something he had heard before in a place that seemed millions of miles away.

"That's it!" Evangeline said enthusiastically, her pink and blue print dress standing in sharp contrast to the more expensive and edgier clothing of those passing through the lobby around her.

"By the way," Grady interrupted briskly, "what was that sermon about again? The Good Samaritan, right? I tried to pay attention, but some of it didn't sink all the way in, I gotta to admit. I remember the story, but not *everything* the pastor said."

"What do you think it was about? The spirit must have said something to you."

"The spirit? What spirit?"

"God's Holy Spirit," she said. "It speaks to all us, whether we are listening or not. The wise ones can hear its voice and follow it."

Grady considered what she said and then continued speaking, "I think it was about helpin' people, right? The sermon. That was what the Samaritan did."

"That was part of it," she corrected quickly like a schoolteacher might. "It's about sacrificing yourself to help other people. That's the difference in life. That's what makes life worth living—loving and helping other people. Jesus did it, remember? He made the ultimate sacrifice and paid the highest price for all of our lives on the cross. He died for us all on the cross. Remember?"

"I guess you are right, Evangeline. I guess that's the difference," Grady said, acknowledging like a little child. "If we cain't help each other, what we got left? Jesus helped us, so we have to do what he did too, and help each other, and love each other too."

"That's right! You are right!" Evangeline responded enthusiastically again, like a star in the heavens that momentarily increased in brightness. Her perfectly white teeth punctuated her reaction. "But why do you ask?" she asked. "Have you had a moment in your life where you were a Samaritan? Or do you need to be one?"

Again, Grady was presented with the opportunity to open up about all the things that were going on in his life, but decided not to because the situation just did not seem right to him. Even now, he was only holding this extended conversation because there was a brief lull in lobby traffic, and Tony was away.

"I think I have," he responded to the Christian woman. "It took a while, but I think I did the right thing. I just don't know if it was for the right reasons and I think God might be gettin' on me about that."

"Can you tell me more about it? Maybe we can get some lunch and talk about it? It seems a little more complicated than a quick conversation here. How does that sound?"

"I'd appreciate that Evangeline. Let's look at havin' lunch on Monday or Tuesday, after the weekend."

"That sounds fine!" she said excitedly. "What about church this weekend?"

Grady thought about all that he had to do and that he would not be home, and politely declined.

"Maybe the week after this one. I have a lot to do this weekend and I'm going over to Hunter's Point to spend some time with my daughta' and grandson."

"Ok, that sounds fine too. But remember that you do not need me. You can talk to the Lord on your own, anytime you like. That is what a relationship with God is about, anyway. It is a personal thing. You don't need anyone in between. God says to come to him boldly before his throne of grace. He also offers us salvation through a simple prayer. Do you know about that prayer?"

Grady recollected childhood again and remembered that there was a prayer one could say to accept Jesus Christ as one's savior and he would enter one's life to guide it from there. Through the prayer, one could also be assured of peace in life and presence in Heaven after death, but Grady was not sure if he had ever said the prayer.

"Maybe I need to say that prayer again to make sure that I said it right? How do you say it again?"

Evangeline edged a little closer to the security counter for more privacy over what she was about to say: "Just ask Jesus to come into your heart and to guide your life," she said. "Confess that you are a sinner before God and that you are willing to repent of your sinful ways. You can put it in these words: 'Father God, I am a sinner and I come to you confessing my sins. I also come to you to accept your son, Jesus Christ, as the savior of my life and I believe he died for my sins on the cross. I repent and ask forgiveness for my sins and I now give my life to Jesus and await his return one day to save those who believe in him.'

"It is that simple," Evangeline said, putting an exclamation of confidence on the words she had just spoken. "All you are doing is letting Jesus Christ know that you believe in him and are willing to let him take control of your life. You can do that anytime, including right now, and you can talk to God and Jesus anytime and anywhere afterwards and bring them your concerns. But when you make your confession to God, you have to believe and be prepared to reshape your life so that it follows the ways Jesus says we should live our lives. You might have to make a lot of changes, but God will be there with you as you try to follow him. No one else can do these things for you. Are you ready to make this very important decision to change your life forever for the best?"

Grady appreciated Evangeline's sincerity and listened to her, but he still did not feel the present environment was the proper place for such a solemn and sincere decision.

"Let me think about it. I'll do it on my own, or I will make my peace the next time I see you all in church, which might be soon. Ok, dear? I promise you. I need some kinda help in my life. Just knowing and saying that means that I am making some kinda movement in the right direction. Don't you think?"

Just then a woman came up to the counter looking for directions to a building office and Grady had to step away and direct her. Evangeline waited until he was done.

"You can say that prayer at any time," she said after he returned to her. "As long as you mean it sincerely."

"Oh, I'll mean it," Grady said through a grin. "I just want to do it in a quiet place. I know when the right time will be."

Just then Tony returned to the desk and Grady's attention became diverted again. "You can expect me in church in a few weeks, all right? I promise you."

"I'll remind you," Evangeline Bishop said, smiling back. "But remember everything I said. Eternal peace is just a short, sincere prayer away." She merged into a small group that exited the building through the lobby's double doors.

Later in the day, as he walked to the Market Street McDonald's on his break, Grady acknowledged in his heart that he would make an attempt to attend church again. He just needed to get through the next few days, he believed.

He had also decided to tell his friends everything that had been happening in his life, beginning with the murder, but none of them were there. Telling them would be the beginning of his confession, of sorts. He was willing to get everything off his chest. In fact, he invited someone to talk to now. So he decided that he would wait a while for them. He went inside and got some tea, came back out, and sat down at a table.

Meanwhile, no human eye in the world could keep track of all the pedestrian traffic going up and down Market Street at any given moment, with the pretty women, the skateboarders, the dirty homeless, the professionals, the poor laborers, and the hustlers of every sort. It was a lot to take in, even for a seasoned observer such as Grady. Sitting there, he wanted to be absorbed again into the San Francisco landscape, but for the first time in many years, he felt repulsed by what he watched. He even felt an urge to resist the always-charming San Francisco air, though it would continue to encourage him to submit.

There was a hard, overcast, gray sky encasing San Francisco, and creating a low ceiling. Grady wondered as he looked up if he might be able to touch it if he were to go to the roof of his building. The gray layer in the sky was so defined that it seemed metallic and impregnable. Was he trapped in San Francisco?

Surely God was on the other side of whatever was up there though, whether the sky was gray or sunny. In fact, God was making the day what it was, wasn't he? If so, what then was the unusually low and gray sky trying to tell him?

This thinking led Grady to consider Evangeline's words from earlier. Just like he had decided to report the crime, he decided he would make his formal commitment to God once all his current problems were behind him. He could come to God freshly that way, and he got mildly excited about this possibility as he sat, watching the crowds, and waiting for his friends.

He closed his eyes and daydreamed playfully. He saw himself going to his building's roof and tapping on the gray sky to get God's attention. The result would be the pulling up of Grady into Heaven and out of the madness. Grady laughed to himself at such a thought, burying a lingering smile into his tea, which he got this time. He was startled when he received a tap from behind that demanded his attention. Before turning, he expected to see either Walter or Wizard. Instead, it was Bill, who had been missing for several weeks until now.

CHAPTER XV

Bill said he had been in the hospital and he did not know where either Wizard or Walter was at the moment. He said he had been having some problems with his legs and the doctors at San Francisco General had been treating him for an infection which had limited his mobility. This disability, combined with his shrinking fortunes in his favorite city, led him to believe that his tenure in San Francisco had come to an end.

"I'm just here to get a quick cup of java and take a last look at the city. Then I'm outta here." He said he was leaving for good, and going to live with his sister on her small farm outside of Corvallis, in Oregon. She had offered in the past to take him in, but he had declined because the city's pull on him was so strong.

"Yep," he said, having somehow acquired a rustic, cowboy accent since Grady had last seen him. "My San Francisco days will soon be a thing of the past."

"Good for you," Grady said. "Least you got some place ta go. A lot of these people in this city stuck here forever. Like me. Where can I go? I can't to go back to Georgia. Don't really want to go back there. That was too long ago anyway."

"That might be true for some people," Bill quickly countered. "But there are many who just don't want to leave. I was like that. This place had me under a spell. It can do that if you stay too long. I'm not sure why, but I think it's because the city convinces you that it's your best friend and that you can't get along anywhere else. San Francisco makes you think that it's the only thing that loves you. It took a health problem to wake me up. But I will always have great memories. When I get to Oregon, I will see if other cities are like San Francisco, but I doubt it."

"Whatcha gon' do when you get there?" Grady could not help but ask. "Life on a farm will be a lot different then life here. Um sure ya know that."

Bill nodded his head, appreciating the question. "Thought I would do some writing. I've had a lot of experiences I'd like to share. Other than that, I think I'm just gonna kick back and appreciate nature and the animals, like I think God wanted us to do in the first place. You can't find those things here. San Francisco isn't natural. It is fun and it has been fun, but this place is not natural."

"Like I said, that's all good for you," Grady repeated, somewhat cynically. He was a bit jealous, but tried not to show it. Grady had early life experience on a farm and there was definitely a big difference between urban and rural life. He wondered how well he would do going back to that environment.

"I guess the rest of us will have to do the best we can while we are still here," he said. "But we'll be all right. Everyone has to live and die somewhere. Ain't no place on earth perfect."

"You are correct there my friend," Bill agreed. "And if you all ever get bus tickets, you can come visit me on my sister's farm."

"When's the last time you saw Walter?" Grady had been wanting to ask before he parted with Bill, probably for good.

"He was worried about you when you was missin' for those few weeks. To him, you're his best friend."

"I haven't seen him or Wizard since I got discharged from the hospital. I was hoping they might be here today. I want to see them before I leave for good. I just got out yesterday and I'm staying with a guy I met at the hospital. I haven't even been by the shelter yet. I'll probably go by there after I leave here."

Then Grady could see Bill thinking quickly. "But if you do see Walt, tell him what I said and that I'm sorry I missed him," Bill said.

With that, Grady felt that something was coming to an end for all of them. He had wanted to tell all three of them about the events that had transpired in his life in recent months, but he would miss the opportunity. It just did not seem appropriate now. He needed for all three of them to be there. The sharing of his information with them, his friends, would be too late. He had blown the chance to talk to them weeks ago, when his life really started to go through changes.

"Well, I got to get back to work myself," he said regrettably and tiredly, realizing all that he would have to do later. Thinking about it made him a little peeved over that fact that he felt he was being chased out of his apartment. However, he didn't want to get into that with Bill. Whatever was going to happen for all of them was going to happen, one way or another.

"You take care of yourself Bill. We gonna miss you around here," he said, before heading back to work. As he stood up, the sun came out and Bill was basking under it on the outdoor patio. He had seemed to find the peace that eluded Grady lately.

Grady would have to catch up with Walter and Wizard later. At that time, he would find out whether Bill had caught up with Walter or not. If not, he would at least help Walter solve the mystery over his friend's disappearance. They were black and white and had a unique friendship that was born of struggle and cooperation.

Perhaps that was the key to racial harmony: mutual struggle, teamwork, and cooperation. He had seen this in Bill and Walter's relationship since he had known them. Their different backgrounds notwithstanding, he had seen them laugh and joke together and try to survive the streets of San Francisco together, often scraping to get through the days and sacrificing for one another. They generally maintained positive attitudes, together and apart, and they were probably better off for having known each other over the years.

The remainder of the afternoon, Grady's mind was again preoccupied with the unusual course that his life had taken in recent weeks. He was comfortable with his routines, which hadn't changed for years. Now, suddenly, change was all around him.

McTeague, the lumbering building manager, was arrested for some mysterious crime that Grady could not determine. This happened a few nights after he met Frank and Owens for the first time. Apparently there had been a warrant out for the big man's arrest for several years and one officer had noticed him in Grady's building. It turned out he had been hiding there in plain sight, but Grady was never told the nature of his crime. He had yet to see his replacement, though building management recently left notes at tenant doors announcing that a new manager would be in place soon.

Lorraine had been stabbed by the Hispanic wife, he had witnessed a murder, his apartment, previously a haven, had been broken into, and he had been threatened. There was an intersection of too much malevolence, he thought, and maybe it might be time for him to leave San Francisco as well, like Bill.

Then there was Evangeline with all her church talk. Surely there was some connection in it all, but one thing at a time. He wasn't completely ready to join the church with all this other stuff so unsettled in his life. He would probably go again, but might not be ready to join. He only wanted to concern himself with practical stuff because he might have to testify soon against some crazy Australian who might have caused his apartment to be invaded last night. The voice last night was not Australian, but the man might have been sent. The police would have to determine that.

Then there was the reward. Jennifer Chen certainly seemed sincere and he was sure that she would deliver on her promise. Were not all Chinese people sincere? That had been his experience and what made them different from black and white Americans in his mind, but he would first have to take part in the man's prosecution because the reward depended on that.

What about this foreigner? Why did he have such free reign in America, coming and going and working as he pleased? It was because he was a foreigner. That was it. Foreigners had more rights these days than "regular" Americans, especially the white ones.

Grady cleaned up his apartment as best he could, but there was still lingering evidence of the break-in and this continued to make him feel uncomfortable in his own home.

He was also still a little angry. *What if that fool comes back next week?* he thought. *I should have something waiting for him next time,* he added, briefly envisioning some kind of weapon in his hand. He did not rule out acquiring a firearm of some sort after his brief stay with his daughter over the weekend.

Out loud, he mumbled, "Ain't nobody gonna force me outta my own place. This is just a one-time thing until we get all this straightened out for good."

Late that afternoon, between the time he finished packing and the time he was ready to catch the bus to his daughter's, he tidied up some more. By the time he was ready to leave, the place looked as if nothing had ever happened. After locking the window and turning off the light, he made his way out into the hallway into the darkness. The sun was still shining, but there was no window in the hallway and McTeague had not been replaced yet by the building owners. Therefore, he was careful, vowing as he entered the hall to pick up some light bulbs when he returned from his daughter's on Sunday evening. He would have the bulbs ready when the new building manager repaired the apparently faulty wiring.

He stopped briefly to lean his ear to Lorraine's door, listening for sounds that she had returned from the hospital. He heard nothing, so he took a chance and knocked. He really didn't have time to talk to her and didn't want any more details about her interactions with the Hispanic family, but he was still curious if she was alright and if she had been allowed to return home.

There was no response.

Grady thought to himself that the wound might have been more serious than Lorraine had indicated, and he was glad that he had called the ambulance and pushed her to go to the hospital. He would catch up with her when they both got back. Like Bill, Walter, and Wizard, he cared about Lorraine also.

As he left his building for a second visit to his daughter's in a little over a month, he had strange feeling that he might be leaving his building for the last time. The feeling shook him for a moment, but he disregarded it as being silly. After all, he was only just going across town for a few days. No one that did not know him could find him there.

The bus ride to his daughter's was not as bad as the last trip. This was surprising, especially considering that he now rode to his destination during the lingering moments of rush hour. One might expect greater social tension and instability on a Friday evening, but that was not the case.

The weekday working people were creatures of daily routines and habit. Their behavior going home at the end of the work week was settled and practical. Everyone was too pre-occupied with the cares in their own lives to annoy one another and they were all looking forward to getting home.

On the weekends, on the other hand, boredom or malaise often caused people to seek out different and more mischievous and dangerous types of behavior to engage themselves. They would not make the best choices often. Weekends were not all they were cracked up to be. If they were not boring, they were dangerous, or vice versa.

So Grady just sat back and enjoyed the ride, watching the people in the streets crawl in and out of visible space. When he got to his destination, he again had to walk the two blocks up the hill to his daughter's, this time with a bag in hand and also with darkness approaching.

He had anticipated the walk, and to get ready for it, he paused and got his breath before making his attempt. As he started his climb, it seemed even harder, making him wonder again about the state of his health. Was it his heart or his lungs? It definitely had something to do with his ability to take in enough oxygen to get good, deep breaths.

The neighborhood, already blighted in many ways from neglect, looked even more ominous in the settling twilight. He was about to enter the realm of dispossessed, tarnished black people, several generations removed from slavery, with no voices in the public square. Some, but not all, were barely educated, many felt unloved and unwanted, and in many real ways, they were society's human refuse. He had not spent extended time among this kind in a while and now he was looking at them face-to-face, as he struggled up the hill.

They generally wore all black, some with shining teeth of gold or silver, and strangely dreadlocked hair. They wanted to be menacing and to that effect, Grady believed that some of them carried weapons. They knew intuitively how they were perceived by society at large and they worked to live up to society's perceptions of them. They acted and looked physically ugly because that is how they thought society saw them anyway.

Though he was linked to this set by the color of his own skin, some of the youth looked frightening to him, with his generally more conservative and matured appearance. Still, he maintained his bearing as groups of the young men, with no apparent purpose, hung out at intersection corners that he crossed, eyeing him suspiciously and shamelessly. Ironically, his greatest defense now was perhaps that he was old and weak, weaker than them at least. He sensed from their attention that if he had been a younger, stronger stranger, he might have been challenged and had to explain his presence in this particular neighborhood, or face the consequences.

Though their behaviors, beliefs, and attitudes seemed a world apart from those of his youth in the South, young people were still young people. People were always people, regardless of the generation. All people wanted attention and power of some sort and all young people wanted the freedom to do what they wanted, so Grady let them be, and minded his own business. He would not be in this neighborhood that long anyway.

About a block away from his destination, after he had reached the summit of the notorious hill, the sounds of music began to fill the air. It was rap music, like some sinister, urban mantra or chant. It began as deep, penetrating thuds of sound energy, followed up shortly and peppered by the rapid staccato ramblings in a voice that spoke of things Grady could not understand. To him this "music" was on the level of that which he heard coming from Spike's apartment in its bombast, force, and penchants for destruction and chaos.

Grady had heard rap music before, but never before in a neighborhood setting where it seemed to set the tone for the area and marshal the attitudes of everywhere it reached. It was as if the music could enter one's soul and alter one's character, if allowed. There was something familiar to rap music, yet hideous and terrifying at the same time. Its leering and brutish beats made him want to quicken his steps to get inside even more. The youth were about to take over the night. This seemed obvious to him.

While twilight was making things murkier and more menacing as he made his way, a large black sedan came roaring right up next to him, rap music blaring from it also. The car screeched to a vicious halt beside him as he stood on a corner, its occupants wearing all black so that he could not see their eyes or make out their faces clearly. He knew that they were staring at him, evaluating him, and perhaps searching for a weakness or flaw. They frightened him, but then the occupants, like demons from hell, peeled off again to the cheers of some of the youths Grady had passed on the previous block. The rap music followed the car down the hill until it dissipated into the air like some kind of audible imps.

"Monstuhs," Grady said to himself before moving ahead. "This country has turned us all into monstuhs." These last conclusions were again drawn from his comparisons between the world he had grown up in as a youth in the South, and the one he was observing now. What was worse? The bigotry and segregation then, or the degradation and descent into chaos by black youth now? Would the salvation for black people in America ever really come?

"Human monstuhs," he muttered again. "No wonder nobody wants to come over here and deal with 'em."

To protect himself also, Grady had his own blackness. However, that might not be enough if he was not careful. Blackness among black people was a shield only to a point, and Grady knew this. It was not like when he was young and blacks stuck together and looked out for each other. Now it could be just the opposite. Blacks could feed on each other like cannibals. All racial unity had been lost. It had happened after the 60s, to Grady's best recollection. When black people got all their "rights and freedoms" in America, that's when they went crazy, deciding that they did not need to unite anymore. But who was to blame? Were the people themselves to blame? Was America to blame? Was not someone always to blame for something?

But Grady marched on, believing that if he just minded his business he would be all right. If some young punk tried to bother him, he would have the proper response for him, showing him a righteousness based on years of hard-earned living that these youngsters knew nothing about at all.

But after the car left, nothing else significant happened during his short but rugged trek, and once he reached the parking lot of his daughter's complex, he felt relieved. There was no rap music and there was adequate lighting so that he knew where he was without confusion. He also got a chance to catch his breath from his walk uphill.

He wished that he could get a glimpse of the San Francisco Bay waters before going inside, but it had gotten too dark. So, after taking the time to breathe in some of the cool evening air that came just off the nearby waters, he knocked on his daughter's door.

There was a light on inside and through the window he could see a large hulking figure coming toward him. He immediately assumed this might be his daughter's boyfriend, the one who was there the last time, whose name he could not remember.

He had not anticipated this, but he supposed this would not be a big problem, or his daughter would have said so. The large, dark-skinned man opened the door. He was big and muscular, with bushy nappy hair and large expressive eyes that were strong and sad at the same time. He looked to be about six-foot four in height.

"How ya doing, young fella," Grady said, feeling as if he were the guest at some hotel. "I'm Ruth's father."

"Yea I know who ya are, pop. Um Chuck. I din get a chance to meet you the las' time you was heah," the younger man said, introducing himself. He extended a large hand for Grady to shake. He didn't say anything else, only opening the door wider for Grady to enter.

"Ruthay!" he yelled to summon Grady's daughter from wherever she was in the apartment. There was no sign as yet of Grady's grandson Paulie.

"What!" the daughter responded forcefully from the rear, before adding, "I'll be right out there!"

Like the last time, the living room television was on. Chuck took a seat on the sofa to watch it. Grady took a seat in the nearby chair.

"You like da Giants?" Chuck asked, referring to the game he was watching. "I like da A's. I grew up in Oakland. But I'll watch anything thas on. You know hah it is. Gives you a chance to check out da otha teams." He flashed an easy smile after saying this, while reclining comfortably on the sofa.

Grady immediately liked Chuck because he seemed comfortable with himself, in his own skin, and that was somehow an empowering quality. "Did ya evah play sports?" Grady asked. "You look big enough. Maybe a little football?"

Chuck smiled another self-satisfied smile. "Yea, I played a little ball for Oakland Tech back in the day befo' da big contracts. But I had too many family proms to take care of to make it too fa'. You know ha' it is?"

"Well that's a shame man," Grady said. "Maybe...."

But before he could finish his next comment, there was a knock at the door. Chuck gave the door a curious look before lazily getting up off the couch to answer it. He didn't say anything, but the look on his face showed confusion over who it could be and slight annoyance over being disturbed again. Apparently, he was not expecting anyone.

"Who the....?" he muttered after looking through the curtain. "Is dis the police? I know they ain't lookin' for me."

Neither Grady's daughter nor his grandson had yet to come out from wherever they were.

Grady figured that Chuck could handle whoever it was at the door, so he did not pick up on Chuck's muttered comment. However, when the door opened and the face of the visitor was revealed, Grady's own face moved from a glimmer of wonder, to utter astonishment.

CHAPTER XVI

At first, the figure and visage of a white man, any white man, in the black San Francisco ghetto of Hunter's Point, was startling. Grady's mind immediately reported to him that the white man standing at the entrance to his daughter's apartment might be a bill collector, some kind of service technician, or, as Chuck had thought, a police officer. But this man was none of these things, and after a few seconds of further scrutiny by Grady, his fundamental curiosity fueled by the mystery of the white presence before him, the unthinkable dawned on him.

"You," he said rising slowly to his feet. "What are you doing here?" Grady did not speak in anger, but ripples of it began to crescendo inside of him. For now, he was simply stunned by the reality of the person he saw in the doorway.

"Mr. Jonas," the man in the doorway said, stepping to the side so that he could look past Chuck. "Like to talk to you for a minute, mate." Upon this, both Grady's daughter and grandson emerged from one of the rear rooms, and now all four apartment occupants found themselves looking at the strange white man, with the strange foreign voice and unusual eyebrows, standing in the doorway.

Chuck crossed his arms across his chest in preliminary contempt.

"What you want here? What you want with me?" Grady said, slowly moving forward.

"Need to talk to you, my friend," the man said. "There seems to have been a misunderstanding that we need to clear up straightaway."

"I am not your friend and I got nothin' to talk to you about. How did you get here?" Grady asked, still overcome with disbelief.

"I followed you over here because I need to talk to you mate." Jack Johansson stood confidently just outside the door arch.

Chuck, with his big arms still crossed, moved aside so that the man and Grady could see each other eye to eye. However, he did pick up on Grady's shock and he instinctively began to feel protective of the older man, the father of his girlfriend.

Grady said, "It's all up to the police now. And if you come near my apartment again, you can bet I'll have something waiting for you the next time."

"Who is dis pop, and was he talkin' about?" asked Chuck, now agitated enough to enter the conversation. He had been looking for a way to jump into it.

Grady's daughter went into the kitchen to mind her own business. She did not feel like dealing with whatever was going on and figured the men could handle it anyway.

The boy plopped down in front of the television, not caring about the details surrounding the white visitor, but he was still listening.

"I don't know. I don't have nothing to talk about with this man," Grady said gruffly. "He needs to talk to the police. Close the door and call them as a matter of fact. This man is crazy.

He killed somebody and I saw it happen." Grady then moved toward the telephone himself.

Upon hearing Grady's raised tone, his daughter returned to see what was happening at her front door.

With that, the man burst into the apartment, past Chuck and directly up to Grady. "I am not crazy, Mr. Jonas." He paused. "And I did not kill anyone mate. You got that straight!"

Grady held the phone in his hand, looking at the suddenly engaged white man next to him, closer than he ever thought the two of them would come.

"Kill somebody!?" Chuck said.

The daughter and grandson were now looking up at the strange white man who was now inside their apartment, directly in the face of their relative, and talking about murder.

With the man's latest presumptive action, Grady now became incensed. He pushed Johansson away from him as hard as he could and then proceeded to push buttons on the phone. "Get away from me and get out of this home!" he said to the white man, whose face was now a burnished, glaring red, to match his still menacing eyebrows. Whatever the man said, whatever denials he had just proposed to the group assembled, his countenance could not hide the fact that he was beginning to show signs of an increased rage of his own over the situation.

While the woman and the child continued to look on in growing wonderment, Chuck, all six foot four of him, casually strode to Grady's side. "What's dis all about pops?" Chuck asked again, now standing side-by-side with Grady. Grady's daughter also stepped up to stand alongside her father in unity and they all watched to see what Johansson would do next.

"This is none of your business, friend. This is between me and Mr. Jonas. We have to clear something up here. Just step aside and mind your affairs. I do not plan to be here long. Just long enough to make sure Mr. Jonas here hears what I have to say."

"Man," Chuck said mechanically, "if you don' back on up outta heah right now um gonna pick you up an' roll you out inta da street. Simple as dat. You feel me?"

After Chuck had sounded these words, the man threw a punch at him as fast as he could, but Chuck was able to duck it easily. In response, Chuck came back up from below to throw a counter punch hard and flush to the Australian's face. The blow sent Johansson crashing to the floor on his back.

He writhed on the carpet for a moment before regaining his footing. "You black scum," he seethed.

"What?" Chuck said, after hearing the man's fierce tone. "If you comin' here for a beatin', you in da right place." This time, Chuck only moved back from the slower moving foreigner to provide space for whatever might happen next. "I met some neo-Nazis up in the pen. You probably ain't no differen' din they is, even though you all dressed up."

But Johansson came back again, attempting to throw yet another punch. Riled, but in control, Chuck hit him again with a quick jab square to his jaw and Johansson fell to the apartment's rug like a stuffed dummy, knocked out cold.

Chuck, Ruth, Paulie, and Grady all looked at the well-dressed and unconscious foreigner lying on the floor of their lower-income home. All were equally puzzled and stunned by what had happened.

Then, with the speed of a dawning human thought, the eyes of the adults in the room turned to Grady for answers, since the stranger had apparently come there to talk to him directly. Paulie, meanwhile, took an opportunity to squeeze the toes of the downed man's shiny, expensive-looking shoes, to see what they felt like.

"This man is crazy," was all that Grady could utter at first. "I saw him kill a man downtown and they want me to testify against him. Now, he's coming here and tryin' to tell me what to do. I never seen anything like this. But then again, this is San Francisco, so I guess anything is possible."

"Well all dem foreigners is crazy anyway," Chuck said. "You nevuh know what tuh expect from 'em."

"We've got to get him out of here," Ruth said, instinctively wanting a return of things to normal, the way they were before the man arrived. "Let the police take care of it. Give me the phone," she said.

As she moved to the phone, Johansson's body moved on the floor and, within moments, he was back to full consciousness. Those assembled watched him slowly get to his feet, after rising from his knees. He jostled his head a bit to ensure the clarity of his speech.

"Rethink what you will say, sir," he said. "I am innocent of all crimes."

"Get on out of here, man. Ya in de wrong place!" Chuck screamed this time in a loud, forceful, and intimidating voice. "I ain't gon' tell you again!"

The Australian left, leaving the door open so that those inside could see him walk into the darkness of the night that had settled over the parking lot.

Chuck walked to the doorway to look after his departure. The police had still not been called. "Uh oh," Chuck said. "I don' know where he parked, but he might be runnin' into trouble if he don' watch hisself. He took a big gamble comin' over heah in de first place. Hope dem boys don't get 'im.

Grady also wondered how the man had gotten this far into Hunter's Point without already meeting the local thugs.

From the doorway, the family could see the white man's back as he walked away, dressed as he was in a fine-looking brown overcoat. He had apparently parked not in the lot of the complex where Grady's daughter lived, but out on the street instead, perhaps to ensure his stealth.

Johansson had in fact staked out Grady's apartment earlier. He had been prepared to confront him there, but had been surprised when he saw the old man leaving, and more surprised when he had boarded a bus. Now Johansson was left to exit an environment whose identity and existence he had been wholly unaware.

As a foreign businessman, he had moved around the city, even the world with impunity. His money gave him a pass into generally any place he wanted to be and made it so the police couldn't hold him in jail for more than a few hours. But he did not know to what extent he was entering completely unfamiliar territory.

"Aaaaaaaaah!" the family heard from the darkness of the street. This was followed by a similar outcry, mixed amongst angry yelling. Apparently, the stranger's presence in the neighborhood had not gone unnoticed.

"I tol' him he was in the wrong place," Chuck said, with a touch of pride that his prediction had apparently come true.

The rap music started, booming apocalyptic rants which filled the air, following an obvious scream of pain from the darkness. The family could not see what was taking place, yet each of them, with the exception of the young Paulie, was speculating.

Fearing that the white man had met some danger in the black streets, an impulse to call the police passed through each of the adults in the doorway, though none of them immediately moved to make the call.

Grady was still trying to sort through his thoughts, as the recent events had taken place so fast and in such an unusual way. He still felt as if he had just finished climbing the hill, and that he still needed to get some rest before he did anything else. The long day that began with his apartment being invaded in the early morning hours, had yet to end.

"Let me go out there and see what's going on," Chuck finally said. Compelled to get a look, a result of feeling that he was still part of some even larger drama, Grady agreed to go as well. The idea of calling the police was quickly forgotten as the two black men, one young, and one old, and both with unique perceptions, walked across the parking lot.

The screams they had heard before had been replaced by a peculiar and maniacal laughter that was loud enough to pierce even the pulsating and pounding beats of the rap music. Chuck knew that laughter; he knew it well. It was the satisfied sound of a young, black male riding the adrenalin rush of drugs and anarchy. Already in his mind he was picturing the scene that he and Grady might be about to encounter.

When they got there, Johansson was in the middle of the street, on his back, the headlights of a car trained on him. One black youth sat on his chest. Others stood around watching. Neither Grady nor Chuck could see any injuries on Johansson from their angle. He looked conscious, but in distress.

The music, which had been coming from a nearby car, was louder now, seeming to vibrate throughout the neighborhood, with its unstable rhythms, profane conversations, and malevolent intentions. It made Grady's heart pound in his chest as he watched the scene before him, which resembled a pack of beasts that had captured prey.

Chuck immediately recognized that he was among the oldest people now assembled at the scene and therefore felt compelled to assume some measure of control of the situation.

"What's goin' on heah, fellas?" he inquired of anyone who would listen.

"Ain't no problem, cuz," one young man with dreadlocks standing next to him said. "Is all good. We jes gon teach my man here a lesson or two. He kicked my man over heah in da stomach. Called him some name too befo' he did it. So my boy came back and cracked him a couple times. You know hah it is? Personally, I don' think he know weh he at over heah."

"Let him up," Chuck said. "He had enough tonight arreadey. I arreadey beat him down once inside the crib."

"Oh you know 'im?" the young man on Johansson's chest asked.

"Jes let 'em up,'" Chuck responded, and by now the people closest to what was going on could hear Johansson growling something under his breath.

"Savage American beasts!" Johannsson defiantly spewed from the ground, having been brought to an even greater rage than moments ago.

He had been assaulted and brought to the ground while walking to his car. He had walked through the young men, who were walking down the middle of the street, and he had cursed at them for taking their time to get out of his way. After one of them had defiantly said something to him that he had not liked, Johansson had shoved the young man who was presently on top of him. The entire group then retaliated by punching him in the face, stomach, and back, before pulling him to the ground. Once he was completely subdued, he was then kicked several more times. There were about six young men gathered around Johansson right now from what Grady could tell.

As they moved a little bit closer, Chuck and Grady could now clearly see the damage that had been done to Johansson's face.

"Animals!" Johansson spoke again, sounding as if some demon were tearing its way out of his flesh. "You should be exterminated like animals!

"See, he still talkin' smack!" the assaulted youngster said, and smacked Johansson across the face again, while others around him laughed. Meanwhile, the rap music continued to pound the night air, mingling with the smells of marijuana that surfaced.

When Johansson struggled to throw off the teen on his chest, several others came to his aid and continued to pummel the white man again with feet and hands as he lay on the ground.

"Let 'em up!" Chuck yelled, to get above the voices and the music. "Dis ain't right! Just let him up so he can get on outta heah." The youth on his chest stood up.

"Animals, savage animals!" the Australian vomited again, once on his feet. "You are animals and you live like animals," he added in an exhibition of mind-boggling defiance.

"I don't think he done had enough, myself," a youth standing next to Chuck said. "White people got everything and still they want more. You ask me, you should give him more of what he askin' for." This young man next to Chuck spoke through a slow, but intelligent, drawling voice. Everyone seemed to stop and take notice of him when he spoke, though some of them could not even see him clearly in the dark. He seemed to speak right out of the darkness, with his own voice joining the mélange of rap music, marijuana smell, and occasional laughter and shouting, in the night air.

"Who cares what he saying," Chuck said, ignoring the chillingly persuasive voice next to him. "Let him go and get him on outta heah. The way I hears it anyway, the police got his number already. He ain't never gonna make it back to wherever he come from, anyway. He goin' ta jail and dat will set dis joker straight once and for all. Believe me, I know about it." There were some snickers in the crowd from a few people following this comment.

"Scum! You black scum!" the Australian spewed once again, as he fumbled for the keys to his car. To some of those assembled, his words were almost like a joke and they wondered if they should laugh. The upper most question in the minds of Grady and Chuck, who had already confronted this man, was "was this man mentally balanced?"

He had been let up from the ground and given pass to leave but—either in his arrogance or because he had been hit on the head so many times—he did not seem to fully appreciate his new circumstances, for whatever reason.

Everyone but Johansson held their breath waiting to see if one of the others in the crowd would react to this latest verbal attack. A few of the more inebriated youth started to murmur about "puttin' that cracker back on the ground."

Of all the people at the scene, only the elderly Grady Jonas could most clearly interpret the racial importance of this moment. He had lived enough years to see his life come full circle, from the hard days in the South, to the mean streets of urban black modern America. He felt that it was now time to say something. Somehow, his heart had been softened by the scene he was observing and he began to feel pity for the white man. He also started to remember the words of the sermon he had heard about *The Good Samaritan.*

A Good Samaritan was supposed to come to the aid of the less fortunate, regardless of condition and regardless of the expense to the helper. This is what he recalled from the church service. Grady suddenly felt that he was in such a position to help, as it was apparent that Johansson was not only lacking any respect for others, but that his colossal lack of judgment might lead to getting him harmed further, or worse. If he did not get help, this man might not leave Hunter's Point alive. Johansson seemed to lack the common sense to keep his mouth shut, but this was a time for compassion and not violence. Violence had led them to where they were now. Grady felt the need to rectify the situation with *integrity.* Where these thoughts and feelings came from, and why they were coming to him right now, he was not sure.

"Let him go, no matter what he spouts off," Grady said forcefully, with the weight of 65 years of living experience behind him. To speak, he had to raise his voice above the jeers and rap music.

"No," came a blunt response from the young man who had spoken a few moments ago. "He just insulted us, and he knows he did. He thinks he's gonna get away with it just that simple. Well, he got to pay for that. They all got to pay for that. We gon' lynch him," the young man said chillingly, seeming to speak for everyone else. Then, matter-of-factly he added: "Right here in the street. Just like they did us in the old days. But this time, we gonna lynch a white man for everything his whole race done done wrong in history, and we all know that they done a lot. They lynched black people. We know that. Now we gonna return the favor. He askin' for it anyway."

A cheer went up among the crowd after the young man made this statement, which they all managed to hear somehow. By now, there were some thirty people assembled in the middle of the street, even some young women, while the music still pounded the drug-filled air. The air itself now seemed to be seducing the crowd and inviting it to violence.

Grady knew this air, but over the years it had seduced him differently through his window. The air had inspired and uplifted Grady, and he realized that these young people were also being uplifted right now: but to what end? Suddenly then, before he was about to get into his car, Johannsson was again subdued by several youths.

"Right here in the ghetto," the young man with the slithery voice added simultaneously, to anyone who would listen. "So when the cops finally come here, they gon' find him swinging from a lamp post and the whole city will know that some niggers did it and it will be a symbol to all of 'em that we ain't forgotten and won't never be forgotten."

The outrageousness of the idea was exactly what seemed to give it life in the minds of the youth. They were no more immune to mob manipulation than any other enraged mob throughout history; and at the moment, the more insane the idea, the better it sounded, particularly to minds that were young and under the influence, as those now.

Both Chuck and Grady were thrown back and did not know immediately what to make of the situation rapidly unfolding before them. Before they knew it, Johansson had been firmly subdued by at least four young men.

Bravely or foolishly, the Australian tried to utter a few more threatening words out of contempt and spite, but he was quickly met by punches to his face and body. In short time, his bravado was replaced by wails of pain as he doubled over in his captors' arms. Though Grady was certain that Johansson was the man he had seen murder Edward Chen, he had not been tried and convicted of any crime yet. What was about to take place here on this urban street was an execution for crimes for which Johansson had no part.

There was a stench of injustice in the air that resonated with the foulness of the rap music and the smell of illegal drugs. Years of maturity and an otherworldly sense of justice and compassion were now allowing Grady to perceive that the stench became stronger with each passing moment. Still, intense emotions were being influenced by the darkness, the music, and the air.

But for Grady, what he was witnessing was not right. So he considered his options again about how to intervene.

"These young boys are crazy enough to do this," he said to Chuck, loud enough for others to hear. But he did not care who heard him at this moment. In fact, he wanted the young people who were about to enact a crime, to hear his oppositions.

"Dey ain't gon' do nothin'," Chuck said with some hesitation in his voice. "They jes' lettin' off sum steam."

Grady disagreed. He felt something ominous was about to take place and he was soon to be proven right.

"Go git some water hoses," the enigmatic young man said again, now seeming to have confidently taken charge of the situation, and Grady made it a point this time to get a clear look at him.

There was something familiar about him, particularly with regard to his stature and the conciseness of his speech. He was a smallish young man, but his age was difficult to determine. From his voice, one could estimate that he may have been under 20-years -old, like many of those assembled, but he could have been older. The dominant color that he wore was black, and that included a beret.

Then it dawned on Grady where he had seen the young man before tonight. He had stood out on TV during the protests in Oakland against the shooting of Arthur Grant. He had been vocal in that incident and had vowed revenge in that case. Grady had seen this on TV, but what was that young man doing here now? At the time, Grady had admired him somewhat for speaking out on behalf of Arthur Grant, but wasn't he going too far now? This was not the kind of justice that should ever be sought.

Along with the beret, the young man also wore round wireframed spectacles that gave him a piercing, intelligent look. Grady had always respected the intelligence of the radical militant activist groups the young man resembled, though he had not always understood them completely, or agreed with their goals and methods.

"Tie em' around his neck," the young man added to some crowd members, after they were ordered to find some water hoses. Snickers of agreement, mixed with laughter, went up after the young militant had uttered these deadly instructions.

After hearing that last order, Grady was certain what was about to happen was real, and that it needed to be stopped.

He turned to Chuck, who was now bobbing his head in step with the blaring music. This told Grady that Chuck's priority right now was not to come to the white man's aid, leaving Grady with few choices. Chuck was now either in denial or in secret conspiracy himself.

Grady, meanwhile, could try to come to Johansson's aid on his own, he could try to reason with the drug-addled youth, or he could try to make it to his daughter's house to call the police. He decided to try the second option first.

"Please young people – young men and young women," he said. "You all can't hurt this man out heah in the street. The police won't let you get away with that anyway. You all know that."

"Ain't nobody gonna know unless you tell 'em, pops," the militant young man immediately retorted, as if he were waiting for someone to contest what they were about to do. He took a puff from what looked like a marijuana cigarette after he said this. Chuck's attention was diverted as several young men took off to various car ports and yards to look for additional garden hoses.

"But this man ain't done anything to you. His people in the past might have, but he didn't. Don't you see that? You can't punish him for something that white people did befo' he was born."

"It's called a symbol, pops," the brash young man responded briskly and proudly. "A symbol don't need no reality, because it stands for somethin'. It could be in the past, right now, or in the future. For us right now, this man will stand for the past. When people find him, they will know that we decided to make a stand for justice – overdue justice," the young man added, now almost in speech-like mode.

Grady felt now that he was in a full-fledged debate. Worse yet, the young man was smart, and Grady believed he could discuss and debate things that Grady might not. He noticed that a few in the crowd nearby were attempting to listen to the debate that had begun between the old man and the young one and this gave Grady the confidence to continue.

"But we got to love each other," Grady implored, still not completely sure where his compassion was coming from at the moment. "If we don't love each other, we gonna hurt each another more. Don't ya'll see that?" Grady could hear some murmurs of agreement, even through the music, and the snickering of the crowd.

"Pops is right," jumped in Chuck, who, like some others, had gotten refocused and mesmerized by the moral debate that had surfaced. "Y'all cain't assault dis man like dat. Like I say befo'— he done had enuf tonight already."

"Naw brother," the young militant said again, this time getting close to Chuck in a threatening way, despite Chuck's much greater size. "It's about sending a message and making a symbol of it all. If you went to school and got some education, you might understand that." His last words, insulting enough to both Grady and Chuck, were made worse because he blew marijuana smoke into Chuck's face.

Insulted and without saying a word, Chuck grabbed the front of the young man's jacket and nearly lifted him off his feet with one hand. Chuck was enraged and Grady realized that things were really about to get out of control. Worse still, the youths who had gone to gather more hoses had returned. They had already connected several hoses together where they got them and they carried them under the streetlights in the image of one long silhouetted serpent. The motivating stranger, however, was in no immediate position to give further instructions, as after Chuck balled up the front of his jacket inside his fists, he tossed the young man to the ground with a mere flick of the wrists.

Chaos then came out of the darkness. Several young men who must have been allied with the young militant seemed to come out of nowhere from the outskirts of the crowd and began to attack Chuck for attacking their leader. They had been listening to and observing the entire proceeding to see how it developed. It took about four of them, but they were able to subdue even big Chuck.

Grady, worried now for Chuck's safety also, knew that perhaps only the police would be able to put a stop to this. But how soon would they get over to Hunter's Point?

As this second group of young men now held down Chuck, Grady ran as fast as he could for his daughter's house, the scene of an urban black mass with possible human sacrifices in his wake. He now had two people to help, if he could.

On his way, he saw his daughter and grandson coming out to see what was happening. They had been stirred by the noises in the street, which sounded both celebratory and dangerous at the same time.

"Those kids gonna kill that white man an' they jumped on Chuck too," he told his daughter. "Get on back in the house. I'm gonna call the police. That's the only way to stop this."

Though concerned for Chuck, Ruth could not help but utter what she believed to be a harsh urban reality: "The police ain't gonna come over here," she said, with a pessimistic disdain. "Don't even waste your time. If they do, it will take a while."

Grady understood where she was coming from, but he believed that the police might come to the neighborhood if he told them that the life of a white man was in danger.

"Just get back to the house," he said, commanding his daughter in a way that he had not done in almost a quarter century.

"No," she responded defiantly, grabbing little Paulie by the arm to head toward the scene to check on Chuck.

"Ok, go on then," Grady said, "but you leave the boy with me. I don't want him over there."

Quietly interpreting her father's meaning, Ruth Jonas agreed and left them both to head back to the house. She did not ask again whether he was going to call the police or not.

After she left, Grady heard another roar go up from out in the street. He reached the apartment door moments later, and immediately went for the phone; but after reaching it, he then dropped it … suddenly and violently.

He had to clutch his chest in pain instead. Then he slowly fell to the floor, as did the phone, with the receiver off the hook. The ill health that he had suspected for months had finally caught up with him. There, in his daughter's apartment, with his grandson at his side, his heart began to weaken and flicker, as the light bulb did in his hallway.

Still conscious though, he gathered up the phone receiver, recovered the dial tone, dialed the appropriate numbers, and handed the receiver to his grandson. With his last breath, Grady uttered the following words to the eight-year-old boy, and hoped for the best: "Tell 'em they 'bout to kill a white man over in Hunter's Point."

After these words, he said a silent prayer to himself, similar to the one Evangeline had rehearsed with him a few days earlier: *"Lord Jesus Christ I need you. Please come into my heart and take me home, and into your presence.* Inaudibly, he made a few other pleas and supplications, before he collapsed permanently.

He had called on Jesus to come into his heart, after the idea had entered his mind in this moment of need, and he hoped that he was not too late. Upon completing his prayer, Grady Jonas died and was immediately transported to his final, glorious destination.

EPILOGUE

When the police arrived, the man previously known as Jack Johansson, was dead. They found him swinging from a lamp post. For him, mercy had not been able to intervene. Unrepentant until the end, his actions and attitude had deflected the mercy, justice, and compassion that is universally available to all; and there was no one in sight when the police arrived, Johansson's body having been abandoned once the sounds of sirens were heard by those responsible for his death.

The young boy Paulie had, in fact, made the phone call, just as his grandfather had instructed, even using the same words. At first, the 911 operator had thought she was the victim of a prank, but the young boy's insistence that his unresponsive grandfather was at his side, and the knowledge that other calls came in that night about a mob, had prompted her to act.

After a thorough investigation of the death in the black ghetto, many of those involved were arrested, including the young militant, who was later convicted of a number of charges, including inciting a riot. However, the exact manner of Johansson's death or pictures of it were never publicized by the media.

With Johansson dead, the details and prosecution of the Edward Chen case were left to the police and lawyers. The police determined that Johansson's alibi had been false and additional witnesses were found who verified that Johansson had not only been in San Francisco the night of the murder, but that he had been seen in a bar in the financial district wearing the same coat that Grady had seen him wearing. There were also several neighbors and co-workers who had testified to the occasionally violent nature of Johansson's temper, and a circumstantial link had been established indicating that Chen and Johansson might have had cause to be working on an international business deal together.

Based on Grady's testimony, his polygraph test, and the other evidence gathered, police and prosecutors became convinced that Johansson was responsible for Edward Chen's death. However, without going to a grand jury or jury trial, the case was labeled as unsolved and eventually filed away as such.

As to his presence in Hunter's Point the night he died and his proximity to the only eyewitness in the case, it was determined, largely through interviews with Ruth and Chuck, that Johansson had come to the neighborhood to intimidate the elderly black man into changing his testimony. The rest of what had happened, including Grady's death by natural causes, had been the result of tragic circumstances.

Grady Jonas was cremated. Ruth had been contacted by a woman she didn't know, Evangeline Bishop, who volunteered to make arrangements for a memorial service at her Baptist church. Reverend Mapple conducted the service and he gave heartfelt comments which included Bible scriptures from Romans, Corinthians, and Thessalonians. Two black men who appeared to be homeless sat in the back of the church during the service.

A soloist sang one verse from the hymn "Blessed Assurance." Evangeline assured Ruth it had been Grady's favorite hymn, and that hearing it had brought tears to his eyes. Ruth was surprised to hear that her father went to church.

Grady's ashes were returned to her in an expensive urn with a plaque which read, "Grady Jonas: A Good Samaritan." She was told that the urn and plaque were provided by an anonymous benefactor.

She and Paulie took his ashes to the shoreline park in Hunter's Point where they had bonded as a family a few weeks prior. She felt like it was the last place, the only place, where the three of them had shared a recent, happy family memory. Although the air was nearly still when she opened the urn, as soon as the ashes were released, a wind came up and they were transported, twirling and dancing not over the water, but back toward downtown San Francisco which, despite its problems, Grady had loved.

Ruth Jonas left Chuck behind for good because their relationship came to feel impure after her father's death. Chuck had managed to fight off his attackers that night in the street. He found Ruth in the crowd, and returned to her home, where they found Grady on the floor, his grandson and the telephone next to him. The police and the ambulance arrived around the same time that night, about a half hour after being called.

About two weeks after Grady's death, Ruth received a call from Spike, Grady's former neighbor, who took over as manager at Grady's old building. She was asked to come over to claim her father's things or they would be given to charity. She and Paulie both went.

Looking around her father's room, she could not help but think about the plaque which came with his ashes: "Grady Jonas: A Good Samaritan." It was a sweet rendering, but Ruth could not decide whether it fit her father or not. Before he had died, she really had not known him all that well. Even though they lived in the same city, she never knew the man he was in recent years.

What did the epitaph mean exactly? For her, the mystery would not be solved, so she decided to apply the positive message of the inscription to her father without judgement. She wanted to think of him as positively as possible anyway.

"I'm sorry for your loss. He was almost like a father to me. You can move in here yourself if you want," Spike suggested to Ruth, and Paulie turned to look over the white man with the bald head, tattooed arms, pierced nose and upper lip, and heavy beard. Paulie found himself taking particular notice of the word "helper" on one of Spike's thick but flabby arms.

"I got nobody looking at it right now," Spike told Ruth about the apartment. "All you have to do is come up with the first month's rent."

"No thank you," Ruth said. "We're moving out of San Francisco."

"You Jonas' daughter?" a perky question then came up from behind them, as they stood inside Grady's apartment. The three turned to see Lorraine, whose appearance looked more proper and professional than usual. All of her clothing was buttoned and tucked in, and her hair was pulled back and neat. Her overall posture even seemed straighter and more disciplined.

"Jonas saved my life," she said, smiling at the three of them. "I am sad to see him go. He was a good neighbor. We were here together a long time."

Paulie now looked the white woman over curiously, as he had with Spike, and others, since coming to this part of town. He was not exactly sure why they were there, but he knew it had something to do with his grandfather. He had been told that his grandfather had gone to Heaven.

"He saved your life," Ruth responded curiously and directly. "How did he do that?"

"Well, I don't want to go into details," Lorraine answered. "But he came to my rescue one day recently and I thank him for that. Thank you, Jonas," Lorraine added and waved up at the ceiling, hoping her wave would penetrate and reach beyond it.

Only Paulie actually looked up at the ceiling to see why she was waving. Spike, meanwhile, was stepping around the other areas of the apartment to give it another check. Spike and Lorraine knew each other but they did not speak much at this moment. The moment and atmosphere were reserved for Grady.

"Well thank you," was all that Ruth had in response to Spike's offer, as she was also trying to wrap things up.

"Sure I can't convince you to think about the place?" Spike said again.

"I don't think so," she said. "I've seen everything and I'll try to get somebody to take my father's things out in a few days."

"You mean we could be neighbors!" Lorraine jumped in again. "That would be great!"

"I don't think so," Ruth said again, politely with a smile. "Come on boy," she added to Paulie and they all exited the apartment, with Spike locking its door. The bulb in the hallway had been replaced by now and it now seemed to have a corona surrounding its brightness.

Spike and Lorraine walked with Ruth down the stairs and out onto the sidewalk in front of the building.

As they were standing there making awkward good-byes, Ruth Jonas was approached by a well-dressed Asian woman, with eager eyes. "I'm looking for the daughter of Grady Jonas."

"I'm his daughter," Ruth responded, wondering what was about to happen next. She had been prepared to get on the bus and get back home. She did not get over to downtown San Francisco that often and did not like it much.

"Well then, this is for you," Jennifer Chen said. She placed a check into Ruth's hands for $50,000. "It's not the whole amount," the Chinese woman and widow said, "but I am sure it will help in some way."

She told Ruth that the reward had been predicated on getting a conviction, but that she and the family had decided to go ahead and honor half of the reward, anyway. Based on the evidence collected and Grady's testimony, Jennifer had been told by the police and district attorney that they believed Johansson was responsible and he had apparently acted alone, killing out of rage over some insignificant thing, as she understood it. They also believed that they had built a good case and he would have been convicted.

"We are greatly indebted to your father," the Chinese woman continued. "Apparently he took some personal risk in bringing out the truth."

Ruth burst into tears, torn between joy over the money and fresh mourning over a father and his legacy, which she did not completely understand.

Standing out on the sidewalk afterwards, the assembled group watched as the sun burst through the sky to chase away what had been, until then, a cloudy morning. Unknown to the others, Paulie looked up to the sky and his eyes also found a small group of people looking down on them. It was the members of the Hispanic family who were looking out their window out on to the street.

The San Francisco air, meanwhile this morning, was filled with a divine aroma that smelled of potential, hope, mercy, and victory. The Chinese widow, the black boy and his mother, the white building manager and white neighbor, all openly and unitedly basked in the things that they had in the common at the time: the man they had all known to various degrees, and the unusual city which they currently called home.

NOTE FROM AUTHOR

If you just read this book and you want to experience eternal peace and salvation like Grady did, then give your life to God. Openly acknowledge God through his son Jesus Christ and ask God to help you run your life. Grady's problem in the book is bitterness, a kind of racism, and a kind of overall frustration with life. What are you facing that is holding you back or holding you down today? Seek eternal freedom and security through God and Jesus Christ. You can do that by saying this brief prayer:

> ***Dear God, I am a sinner and need forgiveness. I believe that Jesus Christ shed his precious blood and died for my sins. I am willing to turn from sin. I now invite Jesus Christ to come into my heart as my personal savior, and to guide my life.***

If you said this prayer with belief and sincerity then you, like Grady, are set for eternity, you will also have the power to be a *good samaritan* in your life, and nothing on Earth can harm you!! God bless you, read your Bible regularly, attend church, and thanks for reading this tale of a man who found blessing, compassion, and salvation in chaos!!

Made in United States
Troutdale, OR
11/22/2024

25168303R00152